# Fairy Tales
# and
# Poison

January 13, 2012

# Fairy Tales and Poison

*A self-help tale, entailing the emotional rollercoaster of a relationship cursed by alcoholism.*

## JENNIFER LYNN BROWN

authorHOUSE®

*AuthorHouse™*
*1663 Liberty Drive*
*Bloomington, IN 47403*
*www.authorhouse.com*
*Phone: 1-800-839-8640*

*First published by AuthorHouse    06/21/2011*

*ISBN: 978-1-4634-2809-9 (sc)*
*ISBN: 978-1-4634-2808-2 (ebk)*

*Printed in the United States of America*

*Any people depicted in stock imagery provided by Thinkstock are models, and such images are being used for illustrative purposes only.*
*Certain stock imagery © Thinkstock.*

*This book is printed on acid-free paper.*

*Because of the dynamic nature of the Internet, any web addresses or links contained in this book may have changed since publication and may no longer be valid. The views expressed in this work are solely those of the author and do not necessarily reflect the views of the publisher, and the publisher hereby disclaims any responsibility for them.*

# CHAPTER ONE

STICKY, WET SWEAT POURED over Hope Morrison when she woke from a half-dazed slumber, only to realise her life wasn't just a bad dream. She felt cold, like when you first open the door in the winter; that bitter, bone-chilling, down-to-the-spine type of cold. Her whole body shivered. As she attempted to quietly sneak over to the furnace panel in the hall near her bedroom, where she could turn the heat up a few notches, she stubbed her toe on a high-heeled shoe that brought back a replay of last night's vicious turmoil.

The shoe had been the object of choice for Hope's boyfriend, Victor, when he searched for something to throw at her in the heat of an argument. Argument might be too light of a word to describe the nightmare that had unleashed itself just hours ago in the couple's bedroom. When Victor had come home drunk in the wee hours of the night, Hope flew off the handle at him in a frustrated rage of worry and anger, which was unfortunately, a typical occurrence of their lives recently. The rest of the night, however, took a turn for the worse, and not so of-the-ordinary. All hell broke loose.

Victor had never physically hurt Hope, but on this particular night, his anger, which was escalated by his intoxication, took control, and Hope saw the ugliest side of a man she had once loved so deeply. It wasn't that she didn't love him anymore, but more-so just the fact that she felt as if she didn't know him anymore. She didn't know where the Victor she had fallen in love with had gone, and she certainly was not fond of his replacement clone. She actually felt a slight hatred towards this beast that had taken over the body of her beloved Victor, whom she missed so desperately.

Victor was wearing a mask. His mask concealed the true Victor, and his authentically generous heart. The real Victor could never, not in a million years, treat anyone as bad as this masked mutant treated Hope these days. Not even a dog deserved to be treated so terribly, and left to feel completely exploited, degraded, and humiliated, not to mention broken. Hope just wished she could force Victor back into love with her, as stupid as she knew that sounded. Communication no longer existed. Arguments, fights, and blame were everyday events instead. When they weren't fighting, there was silence. You could almost taste the tension. Hope envisioned herself standing in a crowded room, and unlike the olden days, Victor didn't even see her. He looked right at her, made direct eye contact, but she didn't stand out to him anymore; it was as if he didn't recognize her. He just gave her a blank expressionless glance. She was just another person in the room; another needle in the haystack of their lives.

Hope knew that one day Victor would reflect back and finally realise the impact of his words; the coldness, the sharpness, and the foulness that seeped from his mouth. She knew his real spirit would find its way back, but the question was, when? How long? Victor never thought before he spoke. He was so short-fused and irritable these days. Another form of pain for Hope was the void of what once was. Every day that went by without his touch, without a kiss, without a peep, just made it worse for Hope. The silence was just as treacherous as the screaming and yelling and madness. Strangers in the same house. The word love was losing its meaning for them. The rare times they did use it, it sounded so fake, so forced, and so questionable, as if they were asking themselves, like an illusion, not allowing the reality to escape that maybe, just maybe, they were kaput, finished . . . done. Victor inflicted so much pain upon Hope, leaving her so hopeless, that even the natural task of breathing took such immeasurable effort and fight.

Hope envisioned a picture of herself, one of her best captured photos, of happiness. This was a photo she actually liked, one of those where she felt cute, with her piggy-tail braids, and a youthfulness about her. In the photograph, she was full of life and expression, and Victor too had once told Hope this was one of his favorites of her. The present imagine in Hope's mind showed the photo all blurred and blotted. There were rip marks, scratch marks, and scribbles, as if someone had been tearing at her, and trying to color away her image. The blotted fuzziness was how hope felt as a person these days. Her own self-image was distorted, and she didn't like herself much anymore. Not inside or out. Her happiness only came in a small dose these days, a very miniscule version of the vitality she once owned with such extremity. There was one person keeping her spirits bright, and that was her beloved daughter. A six month old can carry an enormous impact, rescuing her spirits from the deadly fires of her hell.

Hope certainly didn't feel attractive to Victor anymore, but the issues were so much more profound than just mere attraction. Truth be told, however, she did not find Victor very attractive anymore either. Physicality is only one piece of the puzzle in the true attractions in a real relationship. The connection they shared was deteriorating steadily, slipping right between their fingers. It was physical, it was emotional; it was the whole shebang falling to pieces. Hope was baffled by how little Victor cared about her, a complete turn-around from the love they once shared, and she could not understand how easily he seemed to walk away last night, and just disregard her pain, especially after they attacked each other like a couple of savage animals. She was so desperately trying to get his attention, and nothing worked anymore . . . nothing. She felt very un-loved by the stranger who lived with her, and fathered her child.

Hope felt her own personality was tainted too. She missed her own old happy, vibrant, free-spirited self. She was so full of anger and bitterness. She definitely was not innocent in the violence that had festered, like an open wound, oozing with infection, just waiting to burst in exasperation. The fight that broke out was definitely a two-way street of verbal bashing that somehow evolved into a huge mess that could have landed them both in jail if someone had walked in, or much worse. The backlash could have wounded even an innocent bystander.

Viewer discretion would have been advised, without a doubt, with a rating of a big, bold 'R'. Hope was thankful it stopped before getting overly out of hand, though in her books, out of hand was an understatement.

Hope could only imagine worse outcomes though, which nauseated her, sending her stomach into mayhem. She literally had to run to the bathroom to throw up, and as she was vomiting, so was her head, regurgitating the events of the past evening. Objects had been flying through the air, a curtain rod had been bashed into Victor's arm, which was both a stress-relief and then a shocker of guilt and remorse for Hope. This was a side of herself she hated, and was disgraced by. The following minutes were a little blurred to Hope, but she knew they were ugly and dark. The end result was Victor throwing Hope into a wall, like a big heap of garbage, and smashing some holes in the bedroom door using that same curtain rod that had injured him. He then took off in a fury, leaving Hope curled up on the floor in a ball of tears and agony, feeling totally defeated.

Hope splashed some water on her face, as she wondered where Victor could be and where he spent the night. Even with the anger she felt towards him, she was still worried about him. There was that reinforcement of the deep love she always felt for him; a whirlwind of love and hate all tangled together in her confused and damaged heart.

# CHAPTER TWO

ONCE UPON A TIME, which felt like forever ago, there was a happy, fun-filled, loving relationship that existed between Hope and Victor. Victor really had been the sweetest, most endearing young man she had met, especially considering what most sixteen year old guys have on their hormone-driven brains. The guys that Hope went to high school with certainly were not concerned with love or affection, not without a price. Victor was different. He was interested in Hope for more than just her body, in fact it was obvious that he was scared of hurting her, and that he truly did not want to jeopardize her innocence or the real connection they had created.

Victor's sincerity was as clear as the sky on a bright summer day, and Hope was equally engulfed in Victor and everything about him. He had captured the key to her heart, and he didn't even have to try. A simple glimpse from one to the other could leave bystanders 'ooing' and 'awwing' over their love, because it emanated all around them, like sunshine. A truly beautiful thing. Victor was Hope's first thought of the day, and the last image in her head as she would drift into slumber every night. The feelings were very mutual, and together they floated on their own cloud nine. Victor too, was captivated by Hope, and her inner beauty, but also her outer beauty. The possibilities that could stem from their love were limitless. Or so it would have seemed.

They both had such beautiful, big open hearts, so full of love and such a beautiful bond, ready to conquer the world as a team. No matter what they were doing, exciting or dull, Hope was always happy if she was by Victor's side. She could not get enough of him, and he too, was so enthralled by the time he spent with Hope. Boring didn't exist in the vocabulary of their relationship. Then one day, BAM! Alcohol decided to step in, and come for a visit, only now it was wearing out it's welcome, and had taken over. It seemed that Victor was now rooting for the wrong team. Hope could not back-track to when the problem really became full-fledged. Like an infestation, Hope was unsure how to get rid of her unwanted guests, and Victor's drinking was taking a very heavy toll on their lives, especially for Hope as a new young mother. She was so frustrated at how everything had blown up and changed, just BANG, so fast, and so drasticly.

Hope never needed a super hero or a super model, she just needed someone who made her feel loved, and brought a twinkle to her eye, and a sparkle to her heart. She truly felt she had found all this and more in Victor, until the days when he started choosing drinking over family, booze over her, and the poisonous buzz over the natural pleasure they once shared. He started disregarding her feelings, and disrespecting her as a person. He went from a wonderful young man to an indecent old drunk, within months. No word of a lie . . . ahh, the power of consumption! Victor was exploiting himself, and he was so unaware of the reality he was cruising along. Could you imagine a world without alcohol? "What a wonderful world", thought Hope . . . "We can keep dreaming, but that will NEVER happen."

Their past always stuck with her, like crazy glue; the wonderful memories giving her perseverance and hope, but perhaps it really had been too good to be true. The bad memories were starting to overrule now. Hope probably should have seen past the bubble of perfection that she had been living in, and known that eventually all bubbles must burst. Hope feared that the passion that once existed between them was going to take a very opposite twist and she would become just another ugly statistic, another sure-fire separation with a custody agreement and visitations and of course another child caught in the middle. A beautiful love turned to bitter differences and legal documents, the importance lost in the dust. Love vanished. Hope's fate wasn't looking so shit-hot, and it just seemed so appalling and wasteful. Poor Gracie. So sickening and unfair. Hope's heart just kept breaking, more and more, and more, with each of these foul thoughts.

Here she was worrying about him, as if he was a child. Worry was another facet of Hope's routine now, another weight on her shoulders constantly. Her thoughts took her to places of vile ideas that made her cringe and want to cry and scream; thoughts that made her swallow her own throat a little. A whirlwind of love and hatred stormed through her every inch. For him to not come home, whose bed did he find his way into last night? He had to crash somewhere, and Hope just hoped that it wasn't in the hands of some whorish broad who looked appealing through Victors mighty beer goggles and glazy eyes.

First, the betrayal every time he cheated was painful to her; secondly the dangers rung out loud at Hope, like diseases, STDS, AIDS, and the possibility of knocking up god knows who crossed her mind; and third, she was afraid that Victor would wind up dead for messing with the wrong person, picking the wrong fight just for the stupid desire to fight or because he hit on the wrong girl. She had no trust left towards him, and wouldn't put anything past him anymore. He was so stupid, so immature, so irresponsible, so selfish, all the while allowing alcohol to lead him. Was it really worth it? Hope didn't think so, not by any means. "Senseless", that was Hope's perspective on the subject. Absolutely, positively, completely, and totally SENSELESS.

What defines a man, in all realism and when you really think that question through? Is a man muscles, and being able to pump iron better than your neighbour? A champion body builder, ripped up, six-pack king? Does that make you a real man? Maybe it's facial hair and being able to grow that beard out all rough and tough? Does it get more discrete, below the belt, and how much junk is in the trunk? Does that define a male's manliness? Driving the fastest cars, building the highest tower, or maybe just dating the hottest girl? Numbers . . . do numbers matter? Maybe stats, such as; how many people have you slept with? What age did you lose your virginity? Some men honestly feel that these things matter and that they define their manhood.

Being a dad, being a husband, and being the best you can be in these roles; providing love, a stable home, playing catch with your kids, taking your wife on a date, and sacrificing the joy of a cold beer for the satisfaction of a happy family . . . . these are much more affirmative definitions of being a true man . . . at least by Hope's standards they were, but could Victor live up to these roles or was he too busy trying to live up to the first set of standards or a whole other set of standards he had created for himself. Some men become such at a young age, while others might die trying, or worse, never try at all.

Hope honestly felt sometimes that it would be easier if Victor was dead, because then she wouldn't have to feel so disconnected, and so hated by him. Then he really would be gone, not just in spirit, but in body too. Then, she could pretend that he loved her when he passed. Then he could not become any more monstrous and awful, although worse did not seem possible. This was awful, he was awful! With these caustic thoughts, Hope would create her own internal war, fighting with the guilt of these ideas verses the reasoning of the thoughts. She knew that was not her, to wish such horror upon anyone, but rather, this was her pain talking.

Hope was always trying to rationalize her irrational brainwaves. These thoughts were evidence of the damages being done. Deep down, Hope knew though, that if anything actually happened to Victor, that would destroy her equally as much as the struggles she was living through. Hope had tried to fall out of love with Victor, but she had discovered that falling in love is easier than letting love go, by far. One comes naturally, and the other is defying nature. She would never be able to totally stop loving him, never! Hatred, or at least the idea of hate, is easier than unloving. She could still love him, along with this new hate, as the two sentiments somehow worked together, but for how long?

Why couldn't somebody just wave a red flag in Victor's face? Why couldn't someone just holler, "Stop", while holding a stop-sign? Victor was so unmindful of the consequences of every step he took that he needed that type of direct in-his-face action. Hope was not the person to act though, as she had worn out her control. Was there anyone that Victor would listen to anymore, who could intervene? Could anyone give him advice and give him a glimpse of where he was heading? "Why is he so goddamn dense?", wondered Hope in utter disbelief. If only the walls could talk, perhaps Victor could be told what poor Hope was like behind closed doors, as she silently suffered through most of the feelings she was living.

When Hope defined love, she defined it as forever, through thick and thin, good times and bad, just like marriage vows, which she felt were becoming belittled in society. Marriage and love had been made a mockery of. Hope was a hopeless romantic, the fairy-tale dreamer type of girl, and now her fairytale story was turning into a horror film, and she felt like there was nothing she could do to stop that. She had gotten herself trapped in one of the situations she frowned upon. She dreaded the final scene, the uncertainties and unknowns, and she feared what would become of her life if she stayed, or even if she left for that matter. It was looking like a no-win situation. She just missed the happiness that once came so naturally and free, and that happiness she had taken for granted and lost appreciation for. If only she could get back to the bliss, she would never take it for granted again.

If Victor would just come back, and be on her side again, she would say all the right things. She would do anything he wanted, and whatever he needed. She would be the perfect girlfriend, and learn the definition of what that even included for Victor. She would push the bitchiness aside, stop nagging, and just love him again. Stress had allowed them to forget about their true feelings, and now the only feeling Hope was able to feel was the sadness, which she was drowning in. They had both lost sight of what mattered. She wanted him back, despite everything else. To her, that still meant something, and every little memory and smile she ever smiled at Victor . . . well . . . that all meant something too. Love still had a voice in Hope's choices, but for how long and at what cost.

# CHAPTER THREE

SIX MONTHS EARLIER, HOPE had given birth to their beautiful daughter, Gracie Jane Grant, and the father she thought Victor was going to be, was rarely seen. She had taken him as the man who would really be able to step up to the daddy plate. She knew that Victor was great with kids, as she had chances to see him with her nieces, his cousins, family friends, and he had a genuine sense of fun and amusement when he interacted with them all. He had no trouble leaping to their level, and this always comforted her, knowing his fatherly potential. Unfortunately this new version of Victor discluded that child-oriented side of him, and sadly, she felt that Gracie and her were abandoned most of the time. They were less full-filling to Victor than his brown bottles of poison, which he seemed to be in love with these days. Apparently, Victor could not get past each sip of alcohol without the thought of another. His priorities were totally contrary to Hope's. Those lovely little brown bottles were his gateway to escape the stresses of his reality.

These days, there were two things that Victor felt he could not live without, one was his little girl, Gracie, and the other was beer. Hope was nowhere to be seen on that list, not anymore. She felt so insignificant and worthless to Victor now. Hope absolutely adored her baby girl, and could not wrap her mind around the fact that Victor did not have the same sense of loyalty. Their little girl was Hope's entire world now, and total responsibility rested solely on Hope because her trust in Victor to take accountability for his role as a father was fading fast. Hope knew without a doubt that Victor's heart was definitely with his daughter, but he didn't understand the vastness and entire meaning of fatherhood to it's fullest degree. His abuse of alcohol was destroying what really mattered, and it was ripping their family into shreds. Hope was so disappointed in Victor, and this setback that he was causing.

Hope and Victor were falling into the ugly cycle that had shattered generations of Victor's family for years now; including addictions and bad habits, and vices taking control, destroying marriages and relationships and replacing the love that once existed, causing distress to everyone around. This was not a reality Hope was willing to accept without a fight. Fighting with Victor though, was almost like fighting with a brick wall; it might be a lost cause for Hope. Sometimes Hope was so consumed by negative energies that she literally and physically noticed each teardrop that fell from her eyes. She could sit there and count them, but that only heightened the anguish, and increased the numbers she rattled off in regret.

Luckily, Gracie was oblivious to the destruction taking place right in the comfort of her own home. Hope wanted nothing more than to protect her daughter from all the negativity, and keep her living in a naive world of perfection for as long as she possibly could. Gracie was way too young to understand. Despite the wraths of evil, she was a daddy's girl. She lit up when daddy came in the door, and it broke Hope's heart to know that Victor didn't appreciate that love. He didn't use that love as a powerful force and reason to stop drinking. It angered her that he didn't feel blessed, instead she thought he must feel trapped, and probably resentful.

Hope was excited to watch her beautiful daughter grow, but she was also terrified for what the future had in store for Gracie. Her heart broke a little more with the knowledge that she couldn't keep her baby innocent and young forever, just to protect her from the ugly truth of life. Hope knew that life had wonderful things to offer, she knew there was better opportunities out there, and she also knew that it was her duty as a mother now to show Gracie the path to happiness and teach her right from wrong. She could not let her daughter fall victim to this stupidity she had somehow got herself trapped in.

All Hope wanted was a mother-father arrangement that she felt was normal and proper, which to Hope meant a two-parent household, and a happy, typical life for their family and her daughter. Now it felt like trying to hang on to that dream would mean living out some phoney existence, and pushing back her feelings, allowing Victor to continue living like an idiot. The problem with that was that Gracie needed her daddy, and as she got older, she would need a daddy who could focus and be there for her, and keep his head clear and sober. To Hope that sounded reasonable, it sounded normal, it sounded fair, and should not be too much to ask, but she knew that Victor needed help to be that daddy now, and that was heartbreaking. What would Gracie think and feel, as she got older, if this was really just how it had to be?

Gracie was such a happy baby girl that brought such an immense joy to her mother's life. Her kisses, her little hugs and cuddles, and that adorable little pat she gave people on the back of the shoulder, could all melt even the hardest of hearts. Her smile was heavenly; to Hope, it was angelic. Lately, her daughter really was her saving Grace, from the depths of the hell she was living in. Hope had to get out of bed everyday, no matter how hopeless she felt, and Gracie always made it worth her while.

Today, hopeless was only a fragment of Hope's emptiness. She felt numb inside, except for the tiny glimpse of peace she got when she looked at her little sleeping beauty, innocently resting in a dreamy utopia. Hope wished she could join her daughter in her peaceful paradise of fairies and butterflies. "What do babies see when they sleep?" wondered Hope. Gracie smiled in her sleep, which brought a smile to her mother's face. There had to be a god to create such perfection and beauty, especially considering the man who helped in the conception of this little angel. She hoped that Gracie's genetics stemmed from the old version of her daddy, and not the latest version, and so far, that was evident. Even in her darkest hours, Hope needed to believe in a higher power and a brighter tomorrow.

Hope blamed herself in ways, for the mess of her life, but on the contrary she also never wanted to be one of those enabling women that she read about or heard about in situations of alcoholism. She did not believe that she drove Victor to drink, yet she believed that she didn't give him a good enough reason to stop. She didn't help him to stop. She knew that his routes were paved with booze and broken bridges. She knew that his drinking was his choice, his mistake, and his problem, however a part of her couldn't help but think, "If only . . ."

"If she was a better girlfriend, a better lover, a better cook, a better housewife, and maybe if she had just kept quiet," thought Hope about herself. She didn't really comprehend Victor's hesitations or reservations though. Life is complicated, but once you reach adulthood, you just have to suck it up and deal. You cannot be selfish when you become a parent. Hope did not condone Victor's behaviour. Maybe she should have never allowed herself to get so jammed into this condition, had she been tough enough to stand her ground before things got this hideous. Maybe she should have walked away when she was pregnant and Victor started acting different, and no longer living up to her standards. She was not proud of where she was at in life, nor with where it appeared she was heading. She was so disappointed in Victor, for putting them in the situation they were all in. Could she ever be proud of leaving someone behind though? Hope did not think that was possible.

As Hope moseyed through the day with emotions strumming her a bitter tune, she could barely eat. An appetite was the last thing she had right now, as she continued pushing aside water work after water work, but she did force herself to throw together a peanut butter sandwich, realizing she hadn't eaten much the evening before either as her stomach starting roaring at her like a sick lion. Hope had never actually bit into cardboard, but she imagined it was similar to the tastelessness of today's breakfast. She usually loved the sweet and salty rich and creamy taste of peanut butter, one of her favorite quick snack items, high in protein and deliciousness. Nothing in the world felt right anymore though. Not even peanut butter. Smells, tastes, textures, sounds; they were all just plain, dark, black and empty. Not even the scoop of ice-cream she snuck, like a little kid, tasted good. For ice-cream not to taste good, Hope was in rough shape.

Ice-cream and peanut butter are little pieces of heaven on earth, but when cardboard compares, it just isn't a good sign.

The numb state of her body and soul was really carrying a heavy weight. Hope was starting to feel like Victor's Gypsy-like spirit was going to keep him running for the rest of his life. He always wanted to be a truck-driver, like his dad, and travel the world. He didn't want to commit, and Hope believed that Victor wanted to run away from his troubles in life. Run wild, free, and single, with the added rush of a nice chilled beverage. Victor didn't foresee the loneliness of keeping at a safe distance for the rest of one's life. He had made the mistake of letting Hope in, and she wondered what the defining moment was that made Victor step back, and disconnect himself. She questioned, "Why did running seem like an answer? What was he running too, or from?"

This again made Hope feel sorry for Victor, and triggered her to pity the downfalls he had endured growing up. He could blame Hope all he wanted, but Victor was living out what he had grown up watching, and Hope was just stuck in the thick of it. She always wanted to fix his problems, and be his rock, like she felt he had been for her at times. She realized now, she WAS his problem though, at least in his eyes, and that realization was painful . . . OUCH! Just one of many on his list.

She wondered if Victor was resentful of the fact that she had gotten pregnant while they were so young, and that his freedom was jeopardized and invaded, and that now he felt stuck with her. However, Hope knew that when life had gotten rough for Victor months prior to her pregnancy, when Hope had a false alarm, thinking she might be pregnant, Victor was slightly upset that the result turned out to be negative. He used that against her in a fight during a break-up, stating that 'had she been pregnant, he would still be with her, and that he wished that could be the case'. "What a stupid thing for a man to say", Hope thought in agony. Hope was shocked and unsure what to do with that information at the time.

Within due time, they sorted through whatever phase he was having, and found their way back to solid ground for the time being. Now another phase was standing in the way, and

Hope didn't understand what stupid messages were popping up in Victor's nonsense-filled brain these days. Hope wanted to scream in Victor's face, just to remind him of every word that ever came from his mouth in the past, whether it was good or bad. He needed to be shown how contradictory and impulsive his thoughts and statements appeared. There was no consistency with him. Victor needed to hear the phrase, "it takes two to tango", if resentment was his excuse for being such a jerk.

Victor was definitely not the one most outsiders would label the victim, but sometimes he felt victimized. He truly had an inner self-loathing pity party occasionally, and the rest of the time he was overly absorbed in himself. Go figure. He was definitely not easy to read, certainly not anymore, and certainly not while intoxicated. Hope, too, allowed Victor to take that title sometimes, the victim role. He had never seen a happy marriage, or a relationship that lasted long term. She felt sorry for him, and the worse their situation got, and the worse things got between them, the more Hope pitied Victor more than she pitied herself. The more she blamed herself. She wanted to fix him, and show him that life can be happy, and that love can last . . . or so she once believed.

Hope always wanted to see the good in others, and she was certain that bad people came with a story, a reasoning behind their bad behaviour, based on the experiences that they live, and the hard times they have endured. We live what we have learned, what we see, and what we know. Commitment had a hazy meaning to Victor. Even love was probably a foggy word. Once consumed by addiction, and the adrenaline rush that stems from the poison, and the fantasy lifestyle he was living, stopping was tough—it is infectious, and gives a false sense of goodness to the addict. This was exactly the boat that Victor was in. He didn't get just pleasantly buzzed, he drank till he was outright, and fully wasted, smashed, and hammered. He was a binger, who was starting to lose nights and have gaps in his memory. Days were gone like yesterday. Hope was the obvious victim, but perhaps Victor was too. He definitely needed help, but not until he was ready to accept the help. He was ill. It really was a shame.

Hope also knew that Victor grew up watching the soap opera rubbish that alcohol causes. Victor was living what he had watched as a child, what he had endured growing up, and this was his roots, paved with devastation and destruction. Hurt was a regular part of life on both sides of his family, and the answer was always just partaking in another lovely cocktail. There was nothing a good stiff drink couldn't cure. Hope knew this soon after dating Victor, but she believed so badly that he was different. She saw a side of him that perhaps nobody else ever saw. Love allows a deeper look into one's soul, and holds no limits, at least not when that love is true. Despite the alcoholism that affected them all, his family were wonderful people. Their true colors and warm hearts were visible to Hope, as she looked past the problems that were hidden from the public eye. She adored Victor's parents, his siblings were like her own, and Victor also got attached quickly to Hope's family whom she was close to all her life, and needed approval from. They fit together, all of them. They did approve, and they all connected. Hope always saw them as potential future in-laws, with high hopes. Hope believed there was a reason she met this family, something about each of them called out to her, and she held a soft spot in her heart for all of them. Victor was one of a kind in Hope's eyes.

Hope saw the good in his family, as she did with most people, but they were special to her. They gave off a fun, energetic, loving vibe. That was Hope's first impression. She truly enjoyed the time she spent with them, and they became like family very quickly. It would be no surprise down the road that they would be supportive when Hope got pregnant. Luckily, Hope's family was equally supportive. Words that engrained themselves in Hope's memory bank were those from Victor's dad, who stated, "If anyone is going to make me a grandfather, I wouldn't want it to be anyone other than Hope". As Hope fought back tears, she fell more in love with her babies' future grandpa, and her father-in-law, though her and Victor were not married, he was still like a dad. Those words were wonderful, and Hope needed words of wisdom, support, love, and encouragement to help on her voyage to motherhood.

Hope never felt shy, awkward, or uncomfortable around Victor's family, not in any way. They became her second family, her second home, and people she knew would be there if she needed something. She was goofy and vibrant around them. If anyone heard her and Victor's mom talking, they would be appalled, but it was all in fun, as they called each other names and said horrible things, like, "I don't know why my son would bring that bitch home anyway", or "We don't get along", or "Why don't you just go home", meanwhile they would go on lunch dates and coffee visits and chat and gossip like school girls. It just seemed strange to Hope that such a wonderful bunch of people were even capable of putting each other in pain's way. To Hope, that made it all the more clear that their true potential was beyond belief, however, they needed to leave booze behind to stick together and live up to their fullest potential.

They just had some bruises, like a basket of apples, but Hope knew if she peeled off some of the bad spots; maybe a little chop here, and a slice there; she could find there is still some good, sweet, edible apple inside. That was what she saw more than the rest, more than the negativity. Victor was Hope's golden delicious, sweet and juicy, and a real treat, right down to the core. Hope's family was far from perfect either, but again, Hope herself saw the true beauties in them, and she was not naive to the diversity of the world, and the variations of family structure and lifestyles people live. Hope's own parents carried some baggage from the past that stemmed from her own father's problems with drinking in his younger days too. Luckily for Hope, she had never seen the worst, but the point was, it was there. Her family had issues, and downfalls too.

Every where she looked, Hope was learning, alcohol allows no good. That was a message that really stood out to Hope, one that would stay with her for the rest of her life. Her delicate soul had no use whatsoever for drinking, and had just been turned right off, and hurt too much by the bitter sweet liquors that mess with our heads and turn us into something new. It hinders, and destroys, and is evil. The true beauties of a person can be poisoned, crushed, and killed by a simple liquid. Hope was just a bit surprised at how extreme the issues of Victor's family were as she got closer. She loved them nonetheless, and most of all, she loved him, her Victor. Everyone comes with a story, and every family has dirty laundry, and some are just better at hiding their secrets than others.

# CHAPTER FOUR

ICTOR COULDN'T REALLY BE a monster, this had to be a temporary phase that he would grow out of. Hope always managed to trivialize his issues, perhaps as her own coping method. She defended Victor, all the while probably trying to convince herself that it wasn't as serious as others were making it seem. Life can sure play tricks on peoples` minds, like people are little pawns who can just be shuffled around and put back in a box when someone is done playing their game. Victor kept trying to stuff Hope back in her box, after a good shuffle, and a good round, like Monopoly, or so it felt some days. Hope started to feel like Victor thrived off the rush of bringing her down, and leaving her in an even more delicate state. She still got upset when people made snide comments and rude remarks regarding Victor and his bad habits, as true as they were, only because she did not want to accept the reality. She didn't want to hear it, she didn't want to believe it, and she didn't want to admit that the old charismatic love of her life was now disappearing into a belligerent beast.

All the pain she had endured, all the stupidity she had seen, the immaturity, the irresponsibility; it was all too much, and she could not help but vent every time he was around. She wanted to blame herself, but deep down she knew that Victor had only himself to blame for allowing this disease to control him. When she looked at him the emotions were always too strong to ignore and they would gush out, uncontrollably sometimes, leading to the vicious cycle of her anger triggering his anger, and so on. Nobody wants their faults rubbed in their faces, especially when they are weak and vulnerable. It was always a big pointless argument, that probably only left both of them more upset than when they had began. They were pushing each other away, each push a little harder than the last. This was becoming a sport, and they were both going pro, and joining the big leagues of the 'do not get too attached' club.

Hope just felt it was so clear-cut and for some reason thought that eventually if she harped enough, something would trigger in Victor. In her eyes, Victor had a wonderful life, a beautiful perfect baby girl, and her, a woman who stood by his side, and cared for him and their daughter. If she felt appreciated, she knew that the 'bitch' in her would subside. Up until this point, Hope was never a bitchy person. Hope was not the type of girl to give up or give in, and she hated admitting when she was wrong.

The sad truth was that fighting with Victor had gotten easy, and when she looked back to the beginning of their courtship, she avoided fights, hated fights, and would let things go and pass so much easier. Both her and Victor were easy-going, laid back, and forgiving people. They were a good combination, never holding a grudge, and working through differences without distress. Time, and their path in life had changed them both. Alcohol had helped in the tearing apart of these people and the washing away of a strong love, bleaching away their identities as a couple and as the individuals they once were. Victor had become an inebriated, arrogant prick, disparaging the person who meant the most to him. Hope was a worn-out ol' bitch these days. Her beauty had been lost to Victor. No room or need for each other anymore. Their stubbornness was guarding them, and the whole ordeal was just such a pathetic waste.

Hope was bad for repeating herself, rehashing what she thought and felt, and irritating Victor right to the core. She was fuelled by emotion, so she just released. Over and over and over. Her heart was pouring down, and all Victor saw was a woman trying to be controlling, "bitching and nagging" as he always referred to her rants. All she wanted was affection, love, loyalty, and just a partner who needed her again, instead of needing the high of his indulgences. She was so desperate for him to hear what she was saying, but he had gotten very good at blocking out her words. Of course he would blame her, which is why she questioned herself. Alcohol abusers are wonderfully famous for pointing fingers and laying blame, and of course it is never their own fault, so it wasn't Victor's fault . . . no, not ever.

Victor wasn't the only one to blame for the problems that existed in their relationship, but that was a separate matter. The drinking was Victor's deal, and it probably would have gotten the best of him, with or without Hope in the picture. He had learned growing up that drinking is the key to overcoming the bad times, and he would used that vice at some point, when life got stressful, which somehow or another, it always does. Infidelity was also his baggage, at least for the longest time, and by no means should she be blaming herself for what he had done. Hope herself, needed to take responsibility for her own wrong-doings as well, but she needed help to differentiate all these issues that were so muttled together into one big scrambled clutter.

Hope was pulling Gracie up out of her crib, when she noticed a bruise on her arm. It was then, she truly understood the rhyme she'd been taught in school about sticks and stones breaking bones, "but your words will never hurt me". To Hope, it was the complete opposite, and maybe she didn't really understand this poem at all. She wasn't so worried about her bones, or the physicality of last night's fight. Bruises did not scare her, after all, she was a klutz. The words were what kept repeating in her head, like annoying little jingles that you cannot stop, and that was what really cut deep. The poet of that little 'sticks and stones' rhyme must have a heart of steel, a real tough guy, but Hope had a heart of marshmallows and pudding.

Hope was one of those people who goes out of her way to make life just that much easier for others. She would get a twinkling of pleasure by pleasing others, but obviously went under-appreciated most of the time. She was a person so full of love to give, and patience for others, making it unbelievable that she could be so vengeful to another human being, especially that same man who was once the sparkle in her eye. The only reason she felt such vengeance though, was of course due to her great abiding love for Victor, which was so strong and so extreme that every strike he took at her hit hard and heavy, and each transgression was further corroding away at her inner beauty. She felt such regret, for all her wishes and dreams were disintegrating right before her eyes, and she felt so crippled and unable to do anything about it. The emotional pandemonium she was facing was physically and mentally exhausting her, worn thin and ragged, drained dry, and today, Hope felt like complete garbage, ready to be thrown out at the curb. If it were not for her daughter, Hope may have actually given up on life.

She didn't want to face reality. She didn't want to tell anyone what had happened. She knew that she would break and crumble if she even attempted to get the words out. Shame, pity, frustration, and guilt were infiltrating from her loins. Anyone who saw the end coming would have the satisfaction of rubbing it in Hope's face, as far as she was concerned. All the warnings, all the labels, all the controversy was echoing around Hope. Hope did not want to go into her bedroom. Her bedroom was like the postmark of her failed relationship, for there had been no sexual conduct in that room for months, nothing meaningful anyway.

Empty sex; empty sex with the man she loved, that was all she had now, feeling forced and like a chore. Now her bedroom was the war zone, the reminder of the truth was in the hole in the door, the marks on the walls, and for some reason her bed looked so cold and uncomfortable, as she replayed Victor's frigidness. A bed is supposed to be an escape, where you can sink in and let the day slip away, the place where love blossoms and gets lost, and now she wanted to tear down her bed and rip apart the blankets they once shared. She would never sleep well again anyway. It didn't matter if she slept on a floor or a mat, or a couch or in a doghouse, or the street . . . it just didn't matter. Nothing mattered. Nothing, but Gracie. Thank-god for her. The rest seemed bare, blank, stale, and meaningless.

Hope truly felt as though Victor had fallen out of love with her, which is how she felt about him most of the time now too. Those words came gushing out of Victor's mouth in the midst of his despair, the heartless words "I don't love you anymore".

Hope knew that even for Victor, in the pit of his heart, love still existed, but right now it was out of order, and the sad truth was that Hope was hesitant to whether it was too late for mending, or finding . . . and if they were headed down the path of no-return. Sometimes it felt like she was chasing a ghost. If Victor could not get his head out of the bottle, his life and theirs were all headed for tragedy. Would they ever find their way back to happiness? Would she ever love him the same way, like old times, or had he ruined things too much now? Hope felt the answers were out of her hands now. Fate, along with Victor, held the keys to the doors of her future, the future of their baby girl, and . . . or . . . their future as a family.

Hope needed to find Victor, the real Victor Grant, and soon he would come to realise that he too needed to find himself. Would Victor connect the dots in time to save his family? Did he really want to, or did he feel forced into this life, like he was just playing house? He had admitted to Hope in the past, before her pregnancy, during one of their dramatic little break-ups, that he wasn't totally ready for commitment, and that sometimes he wanted the freedom of being single. Rambler . . . . always shooting his mouth off. Gut-wrenching words to Hope, which made her feel like the love that once existed between them was fading. Victor was famous for spouting out powerful outbursts, without a thought, in the intensity of a moment; words that Hope would never forget, and yet, they were so contrasting, so contradicting, as if he didn't know what he wanted or where he was heading with life. In truth, that was exactly the case, and Victor lacked guidance. He loved Hope, but that wasn't always enough. Hope loved Victor, and could not listen to this stupidity that was coming from his mouth. She thought it was garbage, just the alcohol talking, and Victor just needed help to see that he too, needed her. Victor's identity was stolen by alcohol, completely obliterated, and he needed to reclaim himself.

For now, Hope was left with the harsh, stinging words and the hideous look of vengeance in Victor's eyes last night as he had attacked her. She was shocked and dismayed by her own secret ability to be violent, and was left with the question of whether she could ever get past that image and that memory? Perhaps her and Victor were just not right for each other anymore, and maybe she needed to move on to reclaim her own beautiful soul again. She wished so badly to rewind and delete or wake up to find it really had all just been a bad dream. If only . . . Realistically, however, the eyes she had once found so comforting and safe had given her goose bumps of fear last night. If looks could kill, Victor probably could have murdered someone with his sharp and deadly stare.

# CHAPTER FIVE

YOU KNOW HOW ENJOYABLE that first bite of a fresh-from-the-oven baked cookie tastes, just like grandma used to make? Your mouth waters and leaves you craving more, and one might think they could indulge in the deliciousness of the melt-in-your-mouth wonder forever and ever. That is how Hope would describe the beginning of her relationship with Victor. She fell in love extremely fast, and like biting into a savoury cookie, their first kiss left her craving more of that melt-in-you-mouth greatness. Breathtaking. Ironically, this was how Victor might describe beer now, and his thirst for each luscious glass.

In the early days of their relationship, Hope had never felt so loved, so wanted, so needed, or so important, like she was the one-and-only for him. Soul mates. A smile crossed her face as she remembered a moment in which they had cried together. Looking back it seemed silly, but she would never take that special moment for granted, it would linger in her thoughts constantly, like a quick breath of fresh air, in the midst of a rotting wasteland.

"I want this to work so badly" he had said to her through tears. He had already captured her heart, but for a boy to weep in desire and lust for her, now he had her totally enthralled. They were facing the idea of a long-distance relationship, knowing full well at their young age they could be setting themselves up for failure and heartache. Something deep within Hope was telling her it was worth the risk. As she cried with him, they embraced in one of the longest, most amorous hugs of all time. He looked down at this girl who was stealing his heart, and he dried her sugar-sweet teardrop from her cheekbone. Her skin felt so soft, he wished he could massage those cheeks all day. She loved the feeling of his hands on her skin. She took his hand and held it gracefully, stroking each finger. The warmth soaring from these two young lovebirds as their hearts intertwined was hotter than the sun.

All Victor wanted to do was make Hope smile back then, and oh how he loved her sweet smile. He always told her she had beautiful eyes. She likewise, treasured his striking smile and his stunning eyes. His eyelashes were gorgeous, and she teased him that he looked like he wore mascara, as they were strikingly long and gorgeous. His eyes were the object that had snared Hope's heart in the first place. There was an innocence about them, like a lost puppy, just waiting to be saved, and she wanted to adopt this puppy and keep him safe and cozy and keep him to be her very own. He might as well throw away the key, because she felt there was no turning back. She was his. He was hers. The magnetism they shared was indescribable and one that rarely exists. They were absorbed into each other, always excitedly and anxiously awaiting the next time they could be in each other's arms. There was no greater pleasure than the simple idea of just making one another happy, and thriving off each other's happiness.

Two teenagers tangled in emotion so strong, so scared of love, but ready to leap full-force from the highest mountain top, right into it all. They were young, and they went through so much together. They inspired each other and themselves. Everyday living became that much more enjoyable for Hope. Victor was always on her mind, and even on a bad day, she couldn't help but smile when she thought of him. Nothing bad felt so bad anymore. Life was glorious. They shared a once-in-a-lifetime phenomenal bond, miraculous almost. Everything happened very quickly. The good times were amazing, and the bad . . . well they left outsiders asking, "How?" and "Why, would anyone carry on?"

Back then, the good times far outnumbered the bad, and that was exactly how they kept going, and that was the reason they carried on. That was her justification for forgiveness when times got tough. Every time Hope set out on the hour long drive to Victor's house from her parents, which was a voyage she took at least once, usually twice or sometimes even three times a week, she would get more and more excited the closer she got. The last ten minutes of her trip, the anticipation could almost knock her off her feet, except she wasn't standing, she was driving. However, her heart raced, flipping and flopping and somersaulting that whole final stretch, skipping a beat with each mile. When she would pull down the lane to his family farm, a smile was plastered on Hope's face, and she would practically leap through the door if Victor didn't meet her outside. Victor was also ecstatic to see the old blue Ford beast, her little blue tempo car, the link to his happiness. As she stepped out of her cute little ride, Victor fell in love all over again, every time he laid eyes on her. Hope didn't think happiness could be anything better than the days she was living, and if she could have frozen time, she would have, especially if she knew what was coming, in just a couple of years time. Nothing good can last forever.

Time and life would take these two beautiful souls on an unfortunate roller coaster ride, and somewhere between the bumps and the dust, they would lose sight of one another, see different glimpse at different angles, and manage to forget those pure moments of flawlessness and faithfulness. The pureness and love between them would be replaced by distrust and misery, blood, sweat, and tears. They were in for a harsh and unpleasant voyage, and Victor was slowly digging his way to the grave and a pretty wooden box, in a hole, in the ground . . . the destiny that often awaits addicts. All for the bitter-sweet buzz of a good stiff drink . . . truly tragic.

Really, if Hope thought deeply, she had this brainwave that she had an addiction too, as she tried to get to Victor's level. Hope felt addicted to love, and obsessively, tantalizingly, addicted to Victor. He might be a bad habit these days, and just as his addiction to alcohol, Hope was unsure how to quit him. She thrived off him, good or bad, she lived for the emotional dance he pranced around her, while she kept up to the beat, but barely. She was still so immensely compelled to him. She craved

Victor, and yet he starved her of the affection she was searching to get back.

Nothing made sense to Hope about her life anymore, it just was. Victor was so cantankerous and harsh in his inebriation, and all he knew was that Hope was trying to take away his pleasure-filled poison, and she was an overly responsible pain in his ass, killing his fun and imposing on his tendencies to run with the wind, wild and free, doing what he wanted, when he wanted, at all costs. The one thing standing in his way now was Hope, and how can love blossom and continue to flourish with this attitude of a drunken imbecile. She was nothing to him, but one of those annoying road blocks, that you just want to barge right through.

In the beginning, Victor bragged to his friends. When Hope was meeting them for the first time, they would tell her Victor was different with her than other girls. Nobody had ever seen him this way, he was love-struck. They would tell Hope that Victor told them how much he loved her, that it shone right through him every second of every day. He had no shame or shyness in showing off his feelings. Of course it made Hope feel on top of the world to hear these things. She had never felt that way before, and nobody had ever given her such a feeling of empowerment. Victor took a picture of Hope to school with him to show her off to all his friends. When Hope heard about this, she was overjoyed, and felt like the prettiest girl in the world, uplifted onto a pedestal, like a Barbie doll.

Victor was crazy about this girl, and he might as well write it on his forehead, because he wanted the world to know. He didn't care what anybody else thought, or how ridiculous or silly he appeared. He wanted to sing and dance and scream with glee. Victor gave Hope a whole new level of self-confidence with his electrifying admiration towards her. He too felt a warm fuzziness knowing how much Hope adored him. Their bond was unique, and special, like something out of a romance novel. Magical.

Life cannot be a fairy-tale all the time, and there was definitely flaws in Victor, and in their relationship. She was far from perfect herself. Hope had forgiven Victor for more than one unfaithful mishap, where of course alcohol had been involved. Drinking, lying, cheating, deceiving, breaking dreams, breaking promises, and tearing down self-worth . . . . slowly the nightmare unfolded, interrupting the amazement Hope and Victor began as, putting a damper on their heavenly travels. Forgiveness always followed the downfalls. Hope was an optimist, to an extreme. She was an overly-forgiving, easily taken-advantage-of kind of a girl, who just didn't know how to ever let go, not even when the signs were right in front of her. It becomes hard to see the clearness of life when you get so stuck in a clouded fog.

Eventually Hope would start to question though, could Victor, besides having a problem with drinking, also have a sex addiction, like some sort of nymphomaniac syndrome, a mental illness that was allowing hormones to override his own morals and sense of right and wrong? It seemed likely, as Victor had a tendency to be a bit of a pervert, sometimes humorously, and other times extremely inappropriately in Hope's opinion. He talked about provocative stuff all the time, like sex and nudity, and just talked dirty and inappropriate. Victor pissed her off, and as much as she disliked things about him, and disagreed with several of his mannerisms, and was now learning his faults more and more, Hope just could not stop loving him.

Every time the drama unfolded, the end result was kiss and make-up and an over-the-top mushy, lovey-dovey scene. Victor knew how to butter her up. Deep in the core of Hope's self, distrust and distress never completely subsided. Her suspicions were eating away at her, and each time they were confirmed, it was blunt trauma to her very essence. The other issue was the fact that Victor always left out parts of the story. He could never just come clean with the whole truth. Hope would ask questions, and be unsatisfied with the answers. Sometimes his stories did not add up, as Hope analyzed everything under a microscope, and she would always wonder in her mind if there was more. Months would pass and he would reveal more details, and little twists in the story, and crush Hope more and more. Blow, blow, blow, BANG! The hammer just kept taking another strike at her, just when she was recovering from the previous blow.

Victor sincerely felt bad every time he committed these offences, but the problem was, he didn't live up to his promise to change and smarten up. His changes were always temporary, just long enough for Hope to build back some trust, then WHAM! Back down it tumbled, like a tower of blocks that a child spends hours on. When he promised Hope, he also promised himself. The sad truth was that Hope wasn't the only one being hurt. Victor was deceiving himself, and breaking inside more and more with each foolish mistake. He really didn't even know himself anymore, and he wasn't sure he liked himself either. He wanted a clean slate for himself sometimes, to go back, and do things properly, but it always felt too late. He just didn't know how to be decent, without screwing up and placing pain. He had deteriorated his self-worth to the point where it was numb, and it was almost as though it became easy to carry on with mistakes, negativity, and disgrace.

The mornings following Victor's nights-out were filled with annoyance and frustration for Hope. He was so dysfunctional and useless when he was hung-over, and even more lazy than usual. It was like Hope had a second, older, bigger kid to look after. She would ignore him for a little while, as he stayed in bed and continued to sleep. Sometimes she would make noise, or try getting him up and out of bed, enticing him with breakfast and coffee, if she was in a good mood, and just nagging at him when she was fed up, but often to no avail regardless of how she attempted to perk him up.

Even if he did get up, Victor would slump around on the couch, looking rough and ragged, big dark circles and bags around his eyes, a sickly look to his face and a miserable grumbly attitude which only worsened Hope's mood. He was in the way, if she was trying to clean, and he certainly didn't help to look after Gracie when he was like this. By the time he found the energy to shower and get mobile for the day, he was often called away to drink some more by one of his partners in crime. He was being pulled farther and farther away, and yes there was some peer pressure and outer influences in his friends and even family members, but Victor could stand up for himself, when he really wanted. He just didn't want to be there anymore. This was just stupidity.

Victor no longer acknowledged Hope's feelings. She, as a person, did not hold value to him any longer. This was another huge loss to Hope, on the list with everything else she felt vanished from her life. All fundamental pieces of her puzzle, abducted from under her nose. Victor had a younger brother, whom Hope knew looked up to him, and Hope also had a younger brother, who idolized Victor in ways, and Hope just prayed that these boys never followed in Victor's footsteps. Women deserve respect and dignity, and should be treated as equals. Women are people, not doormats to walk across and wipe dirty boots on. Hope also hoped that Victor's little sister never fell for an idiot like her big brother. She feared the worst for his sister, only because typically these story lines are repetitious, and a cycle of failure. She was similar to her mother in many ways . . . would this be one of them too?

Victor's family was filled with so many great, wonderful, terrific people, so loving and caring, and genuinely humble people. If they could forget about their binges, their futures would all be brighter. Hope just wished she could eliminate the drinking, and see where their paths would all lead. Instead they created such rifts and fumbles, and became all too good at hurting their loved ones, and especially the people who they loved most. Their best friends and closest ties were the first ones shot down when the buzz was at its best. Bonds were being broken every way you turned.

# CHAPTER SIX

ICTOR HAD TRIED TO quit drinking, and a big part of him beyond a doubt really wanted to stop, but alcohol and the abuse of alcohol was such a norm in the way Victor grew up. Alcoholism ran in Victor's family. He was haunted by the shadows of his family, a bitter-sweet life. His own parents' marriage had been broken by lies, cheating, and booze! Victor had vowed to himself never to follow that road. He couldn't accept that he might need some help getting past his problems, and that he really was struggling to overcome the dependency and the cravings. Hope would try talking to him about the problem, and sometimes when he would set aside his denial, and finally admit his guilt, he would say things like, "I should probably quit for awhile", or "if I just stop when I reach my limit, I would be fine", always minimizing the issue.

'He didn't have an alcohol problem, he just did stupid things when he drank', and in his scrutiny that made sense. Victor would get defensive when these responses didn't satisfy Hope, or when he could sense her apprehensiveness and doubt. Nobody could even hint that he had an alcohol dependency issue, because he had all the answers, stating, "Alcoholics drink all the time, and they can't stop . . . if I want to, I can stop", said a hard-nosed Victor, on numerous occasions.

Of course when Hope heard this, she would have the nerve to say, "Well then quit, you idiot". Heaven forbid she suggest that because when Victor was told what to do, he would lash out, like a child, and he would do the exact opposite. Nobody was going to undermine him or boss him around. Nobody could tell

Victor Grant what to do. This was the frustrations and ugliness Hope faced repetitively, on a daily basis. Child-like and petty. If she said nothing, maybe, just maybe, he would stop on his own terms and his own will, but how could she realistically stand by in silence.

Victor had stopped for an entire six months once before, but he was only about seventeen at the time. In reality, he should not have been drinking yet, legally, but of course kids will be kids. The problem was already sneaking up on him. Victor was drinking at a very young age, and by the time he reached a legal bar age of eighteen, he was primed and ready to cause a stir. That was his entrance into the life he thought was so cool, containing 'hot chicks', booze, booze, and more booze, and his gate to fame, leaving Hope and her feelings in the dust. She became a burden, in the way of this new lifestyle he envisioned, based on the carrying-ons his father had bragged about. Victor was blacking out most nights after he drank, and all the fun was forgotten the very next day, and really, that should not have been worth anything to him anymore. How is that even fun . . . well, that probably should have been his warning, but he did not see it that way. Nothing works out that easily.

"I'll show her", he thought. With that, he was off like a shot, ready to indulge in his cold bubbly sanctuary of drunken wonder. Again, and again, and again. Hope had apparently wasted her breathe, yet again, and was left to feel worthless, since she could see the stupid games Victor was playing, and he had no concern for her feelings. Making her jealous was even a wee tiny bit enjoyable. He got some sick pleasure from her weakness, because he still had the upper hand in the matter.

Hope would try to have a conversation with Victor regarding the topic of his drinking in a manner of reaching out, and not searching for a fight. Victor was hell-bent on avoiding the subject, and ignoring the danger signs. He would get explosively defensive as time went on, and had developed a nasty temper, despite the fact that Hope had originally fallen in love with his laid-back nature. Hope blamed herself for his temper, just as an enabler does, when realistically she would learn that this is a tendency of someone with an alcohol problem. Her temper was not always the prettiest sight either.

Hope loved to write, and used it as a therapeutic technique for coping, and often tried reaching out to Victor in a more apologetic nature through writing, professing her still-existent love for him, in hopes of triggering some type of emotion. She wanted him to see what she saw, and feel what she felt. They used to be on the same page, but now it was impossible. She hoped he would stop drinking, for her sake, and the sake of them. She would highlight some of their best times in her letters, but the response was never what she wanted. Oh, how alcohol changes a person. Everything that had magnetized them to each other in the first place was different now, and disappearing, without a trace.

Now Hope walked on eggshells around Victor, second guessing the seriousness of his situation. She was supposed to sit back and watch the person she loved most ruin his life, which in turn meant her life and the life of their young daughter were all in ruins together. She could not allow that, not in silence. She had inadvertently allowed herself to get trapped in the drama, and even feed off the chaos, because sometimes living in chaos is better than not feeling anything at all. That can only work for so long though. There is always an ending point in these types of situations. Destruction and suffering take their toll on a body. The question was, when would it end, and how . . . happily, or not? To anyone watching, the whole case spelled out no-good, but Hope was reluctant to throw in the towel on Victor, still!

# CHAPTER SEVEN

OCCASIONALLY, HOPE WOULD CONTEMPLATE the idea of leaving Victor, and she would toss around the pros and cons in her head. She would even envision life as a single mom, and part of her accepted the idea, while a bigger part of her was terrified of being alone for the rest of her life. Could she ever love again? Probably not, not to mention that she didn't feel she was a big catch as a single mom who would have nothing to her name, except a pre-made family. How appealing, right? She hoped that if her and Victor did split up, she would find another man, but that thought always left her sad, because she didn't want a step-dad for Gracie, and truly, when it really came down to it, she just wanted Gracie's real dad to be better and man-up. She didn't want to love again, or love anyone new. She just wanted the old Victor. She wanted her old life, but the grown-up, adult, parenting version of who they were as a pair.

If Victor could see through her eyes for a just a day, he would understand. If he would just put away his macho ego, something would go, "CLICK" inside his head, and he would know that Hope's heart was in the right place, and that she was just trying to make life better. She wanted a good family life, as any mom should. Victor saw Hope as his rival, who thrived on his misery. He felt like the whole world was against him, and Hope was the head of the wolf pack who was feeding off his wounded flesh, out for blood, and out to kill.

In between his binges and alcoholic fun, there was a loving and caring young man who knew how to have genuine un-intoxicated fun, and be respectful, and despite his imperfections, Hope was madly in love with this scarred soul. He did not start out so damaged, but life was taking its toll on poor Victor. These days, even the sober Victor wasn't so kind and gentle or fun to be around, at least not for Hope. Less and less of that kind caring man was surfacing these days. Love doesn't always make sense, and it most definitely does not seek out perfection. Hope saw the good in Victor, and his potential to be something great, and she wanted to save him from the destiny everyone had deemed him to have. She wanted to save him from himself.

She hated how the stories were all the same, so typical, so readable, but those idiots keep poisoning themselves and they just cant figure it the hell out. They just keep torturing themselves and the people they love, and they somehow get to play victim when realistically their the bad guys. This thought always frustrated her, yet she would always reason with herself, and allow Victor to be the victim, yet again, making it easier to forgive him. Her thoughts were always conflicted, and she just wished the answers would hit her in the face. Is it really worth the attention to look like such a god damn fool? Hope just wanted Victor to be better. He was not living up to his potential and it just seemed like such a waste to Hope.

Hope knew the person, the man, the wonderful, absolutely wonderful man who was hiding inside this hostile monster. She knew the prospective for him to be an amazing father. There were times in her pregnancy when she saw how capable he was, and how he pulled through when she needed him, when she was scared, and when she didn't have all the answers. She saw the excitement encompassing him, to be a daddy. Why couldn't he be there now, now when she really needed him to step up to the plate, and be a man, and be a dad, and be a partner and just love her again, that was what she missed. He could not provide her with any support whatsoever.

Everybody knows what it is like to miss someone. People die, people leave, people move, people grow, and people change. Hope knew all-too-well that it was possible to be in the same room as someone, yet still miss that person. That might be the worst type of missing. To lay next to someone, yet long to touch them is an awful feeling. A stranger in her bedroom.

All Hope wanted was to reach out and hold him, to touch him, and to tell him she loved him and that everything would be ok. What would be better? To hear him say those three magical words, the impossible words that used to be so easy for him to say. The words he used to say so happily, so freely, always, and constantly, were missing now. To hear those words again now, after waiting in limbo, would be life-changing and miraculous to Hope. Instead she was left pining for him, with emptiness and a churning in the pit of her stomach.

A few years prior to all this heinousness, Hope had a life-altering experience, but it was through Victor's adventures that she stumbled upon this eye-opening occurrence. Hope learned about human mortality one afternoon, in a somewhat indirect, but powerful manner. Thank God it didn't take an actual loss or a life wasted for her to see this lesson. Hope was startled, and reminded of the uncertainties of life, and how quickly things can change, all in a situation that could have had a worse outcome. For her it was enough to actually appreciate loved ones with just a little more effort and thought, and hang on dearly to those who count. Victor was in a motor vehicle accident that traumatized Hope, but did not seem to phase much on him as the driver and only occupant of the vehicle.

The accident had shaken her up more than it shook Victor, that was obvious. It was a bad accident, but somehow, he miraculously walked away without a scratch. Hope wasn't even a passenger, however she was the first one he called, despite them being on a `break` at the time. Seeing what was left of his mother's car brought Hope to tears instantly, and she couldn't help but feel an overwhelming desire to hug Victor and hold him close. She just couldn't get the message across to him though, and he didn't understand what the event did to her. Hope believed that everything happened for a reason, and was upset that Victor brushed the whole event off.

Victor was going through some ordeal at the time, unsure what to do with himself. Surprise, surprise . . . him and his phases. He didn't attend school regularly, he was failing, and would most likely be unable to graduate with his class, which is how that played out, and he couldn't keep a job. He just had no interest, ambition or initiative to do anything. Hope refused to stand by someone who had nothing going for him, when she was working her butt off in University, and therefore they decided to call it quits. They had done this a time or two, as most teenagers do, just over-dramatizing and trying to find themselves in the adult world. They were different people, and just seemed like they had no common balance or interest anymore. She just wanted him to take the hint and get himself together, and realise that he needed her, but it didn't work to her plan. Instead he used the freedom to get drunk more often, hook up with anyone and everyone he wanted, and make her feel even worse.

Victor had come to Hope's apartment that day, because she had agreed to lend him money, still trying to be there for him, and waiting for him to realise this. They started arguing of course, and he furiously took off with her debit card, to go withdrawal some cash for himself. Blowing through a stop sign, and hitting a City Bus just seemed like a big joke to Victor once his shock wore off, or at least he would never let on to any drastic feelings. For Hope, after witnessing the car immediately after Victor called her to the scene, this was devastating and it loomed over her for weeks to come. She couldn't shake off the thought that he should have been hurt, or even killed, considering the car was completely smashed in and mangled on the front end. Being the caring person she was, Hope took Victor to the hospital, just as a good girlfriend would, all the while, being his ex, a word she hated. She was worried about him, but he didn't seem to be very concerned, and she was so frustrated that he didn't use this accident as a wake-up call. She did however feel that there was meaning and significance in the fact that she was the first person he called after this happened, and deep down she knew he needed and wanted her support in his state of fear.

They were always there for each other through the worst times. Somehow, they got past that segment, and Victor did manage to get himself together. The potential was always there. They found their way back to each other, and sorted the tough stuff, like always. Once again, their love pulled them together, despite the odds being against them. Hope, however, would never forget that afternoon. She believed in guardian angels in times like those. She didn't want to lose Victor, and she knew he was lucky that day, but perhaps his luck would run out, if he wasn't a little more careful. Angels cannot always protect the people who don't want to be protected. Life lessons can only be learned by those who open their minds.

Reverting from past to present, all the while still thinking of luck, Hope wished a Genie would jump out at her, as she glanced over at her teapot on the kitchen counter. Wish number one, simple, "Send me a sign, help me find the answers, I am lost, and don't know where to turn anymore, or what to do next", said Hope out loud, though she was alone in the room. This was a generalized, vague wish, but Hope didn't have a clear answer and hoped some higher power might.

With a heavy sigh, she continued on, saying, "Wish number two, I want Victor to walk through the door with the words 'I love you', escaping his lips." Now this was getting down to business and much more to the point. With another pause, she whispered, "please god, I don't want to sound greedy, but please help Victor find the strength to quit drinking, forever, giving him the guidance he needs. I am not only asking for myself, but in the best interest of our precious baby girl who deserves great things, and also in the best interest of Victor, though he may not see it now. Oh please!" As she practically begged out loud into the empty room, the desperation was obvious in Hope's voice as it crackled slightly. She could really sense Victor slipping away now, and she was so afraid to lose the love of her life.

She then stared at the teapot, as if she actually thought Mr. Genie would pop on out and answer her. She wanted to feel loved again, and was starting to think only a miracle would make that happen. She could wager with Genies and plead to God till she turned blue in the face, but Victor really was a different person these days, and she knew god wasn't responsible for this. This was venomous; this was the doing of the devil. Victor must have sold his soul, and here as Hope was feeling like giving up, crying, as she fell to her knees, she yelled out, "Satin please, you don't want him, he is too good for you, please, give him back . . . to me". She felt so lost and alone as she laid back down and fell asleep again in a soggy pool of tears.

# CHAPTER EIGHT

S HOPE SLEPT, SHE fell into dreams of the past, flashbacks of days gone by, and beautiful memories of times she longed to get back. Her dreams took her back to the first time she met Victor. She would later make fun of him for his cheesy pick-up lines and creepy flirtatious eyes, the 'googly-eyes' she called it, but then she would laugh because despite how cheesy and creepy he may have been, it certainly won her over. They always had fun together, they made each other laugh, and brought out good spirits and bright smiles in one another. Their happiness radiated all around them, and might even be inspirational to others. Even Victor's mother recalled their first introduction, and Hope's humorous charm won her over as well. Victor's parents could probably sense the bond right from that day, as they listened in on a slobbery lip-lock before Hope drove away that night.

Hope had always been the girl without the boyfriend in her little group of friends. She was by no means a depressive girl, and she certainly wore and shared a positive vibe. Her smile was her trademark. She knew she didn't have the gorgeous looks to offer any guy, but she also knew she had a great heart, but it would take her a few more years to truly value that in herself. Society, through media, depicts a very stereotypical, false imagery of what pretty should be. Hope had friends who in her mind were drop-dead gorgeous, super-model material, and standing beside them made her feel below average, at least in the looks department. She knew someday her inner beauty would matter, but high schoolers are too immature to see beyond physicality.

She had a happy personality, and liked herself, but when it came to her looks, she always compared herself to other people and wished she had a little pizzazz. Her childhood was wonderful, and she didn't feel deprived or damaged. Hope had a loving family life; it was just this image of beauty that she held, and didn't feel she owned, giving her a negative self-concept.

Kids and teenagers can be cruel, and school can be a cruel atmosphere for youth, creating a superficial and judgemental attitude throughout society. Hope held a slightly distorted view on society, thinking that a person's worth was measured by their marital or relationship status. Pretty girls and cool girls had boyfriends. If you never get married, then you must not be worth enough to anyone. As Hope got older, she realised that small towns and public schools teach children these stupid ideologies, and unfortunately this is what gave her these perspectives. With time, Hope would learn that these standards were not always the case. She spent two years as a University student, which certainly broadened her horizons on people, labels, and acceptance. Sometimes the so-called ugly girl really does get the cool guy, just like in the movies. Anyone is worthy of love, and finding someone special, and it really holds true when you here the phrase "Be yourself!" Hope also learned that the uniqueness of people is what makes them special. Getting to know someone can really teach us about judging books by their covers, or how not to make that mistake.

Hope's one-tracked opinion was branching, and her own individuality was making its debut, all because someone gave her a chance. She would explore herself, and sail new seas, with unexpected results, but this would be a timely process, and wouldn't come easily or freely. Hope would sometimes obsess and over-analyze her body. A mirror was sometimes her worst enemy, as she stared deep into every line, pimple, freckle, scar, and flaw her face withheld. Head to toe she could find something wrong. Goofy toes, stubby thumbs which she felt looked masculine, and friends referred to as "alien thumbs", and her scarred, scraped, knobby knees that protruded out of her pasty white chicken legs. Her veins seemed to jump out, and then there was her non-existent A-cup breasts, that she waited to watch grow, and that didn't happen until she got pregnant and breastfed. That was a whole new story.

After breastfeeding she would have even less, dried up, negative A-cups, but luckily by that point she would have a new level of confidence that came from within. She could joke with almost anyone at that point, and not feel so low about little boobs. Suddenly the ability to bear a child and feed a child, and be a great mom gave her a feeling of beauty that was dangerously powerful and unexplainable. Nobody else's opinion mattered anymore, not that she was ever bullied, but it was just her own beliefs. Her daughter's smile, and the knowledge that her daughter needed her was profoundly uplifting. She had found her calling, and looks didn't matter anymore. She was proud of her body now, but soon after her daughter's birth, Victor would beat her self-esteem down, despite her motherly glow. She thought that watching her give birth and watching the mom character come out of her should strengthen their bond and his love for her, but it was completely the opposite.

Hope had some petty pre-teen boyfriends, but perhaps then she should have realised that each time a boy paid any attention and interest in her, she was always questioning his ulterior motives. Hope was smart, one of those over-achieving hard-working, competitive type of students in school. Perhaps she was stereotypically labelling herself as a nerd, and therefore not really worthy of dating anyone she would have found attractive. It was the idiots and the assholes that Hope was always attracted to, and she often wondered "Why is that"? In the midst of all that, she still held this vision for her future of marrying a handsome, successful man who appreciated her brains and her character, and not the color of her hair, or the lines on her face.

Hope couldn't forget the ultra-nice guy who came across as nerdy, but was so shy that he couldn't work up the nerve to admit he was stringing along two girls. He and Hope had a short-lived phone dating saga; a one-time introductory visit, brought together by friends. The two hit it off, as planned, but when their phone conversations soured, and Hope sensed something wasn't right, she finally confronted him to find that he had a girlfriend. He had only lied to Hope for the past week, and he thought it was justified because this was the girl he always wanted. When Hope saw a picture of this girl, she thought she was unattractive, and wondered if he thought she was that hideous and unsightly too. It didn't give her much of a confidence booster, that was for certain.

Hope was still living in the eyes of physical appearance meaning everything, and perhaps she should have learned then, it wasn't always so. Not to mention that perception is in the eye of the beholder, much like beauty. Opinion is a state of mind. Years later, Hope would discover that this foolish boy regretted his choice, not based on looks, but just personality and circumstances, and he had a secret ongoing lust towards Hope, one which he never totally got over. At the time however, it crushed her, but luckily she was able to move on fairly fast.

For the period of time when she was finally the one with a boyfriend, for more than a week, it all lead to severe heartache. He was the popular guy, she wasn't quite as cool, and even though he had been a very sweet guy, they had a very strange relationship. It wasn't his fault really, it was her own insecurities. At school, she felt so awkward around him and his older, cooler crowd of friends. She was almost too embarrassed to talk to him, only because she felt she wasn't good enough and was scared of what people would think and say. The internet had allowed her to admit her crush, through online chatting, but as her nervousness climbed she wondered what she had just done.

They went on a date, and she was immediately falling in love, or the idea of love in her lustful state of vivacity. To date her crush seemed surreal and amazing, like something out of a movie. Unlike the movies though, it was not clear-cut, and Hope may have made choices that were not the best. Her shyness meant they didn't really communicate at school, just on their own time, and yet he openly admitted to people that they were together. He wasn't ashamed of her, but she felt that he should be. Even during their one on one time, Hope was nervous, and scared of saying or doing the wrong thing. She couldn't really be herself. She had created her own stigma which she carried throughout her school years. Just as she started to feel more comfortable, and just when it may have become more intimate, that was when they started to unravel.

A popular guy was 'in love' with Hope. He really did seem sincere, and they shared some wonderful times. He helped her to feel better about herself, but deep down she was scared to lose him, just for the simple reason that she didn't feel good enough. Her fears and insecurities are probably what pushed him away. Perhaps her signs of jealousy towards other girls whom he was friends with also played a role. Or maybe it was the fact that she got so attached, so quickly, which was what he pointed out when he was breaking up with her. The irony in that was that he had been the first to say those three magical words, "I love you," which she wanted to hear again, as he told her they were finished months later. She even remembered what she was doing the first time he said it, biting into his favorite cookie that he insisted she try. The cookie and his words were so jointly wonderful, but all too good to last.

She certainly had regrets when that relationship went down the drain. She was a fast faller, and could easily get her heart broken, which left her scared to be in love again. She had practically become obsessed with this boy, and didn't know how to let go, so she vowed never to make that mistake again. She would never fall for anyone again, unless she knew that it was going to last forever. When hearing this story, Victor had promised Hope that he would never hurt her like that. Victor would in fact, confront this ex-boyfriend of Hope's one night when he was intoxicated, which gave Hope a secret boost of confidence, but also embarrassed her at the same time. Liquid courage. That was it though, he had said what needed to be said for her to let down her guards.

Another factor in this previous relationship failing may have been Hope's fears of being sexual, although he was much too gentlemanly to force himself on her or to ever admit that this was an issue, and they certainly had some wonderful make-out sessions that would leave Hope drooling for more. Still, she was terrified for any guy to ever see her naked; she would stand in front of a mirror wondering why she couldn't have a body like a movie star, and hoping that someday some guy would accept every scar and flaw on her. The fact that she was so quick to let her guards down, and never feel the awkwardness with Victor, made her believe that he was meant for her. Not only that, but Victor praised her body, and made her feel like a goddess. Right from the start, Victor was different than other guys.

That first night Hope and Victor were hanging out together with mutual friends, and Victor had asked, "So how does a girl as pretty as you not have a boyfriend?" With those corny words, he was already reeling her in. Here they were in a room full of people, but completely absorbed in each other. The first time their hands linked, a vibration penetrated through their arms, down to their feet, through every nook and cranny in both of them. This is the feeling she now pined for, to be his number one again.

However, years earlier, in their pre-pubescent days, they met at a party, and Victor had struck Hope as a very cocky, self-righteous poser, who was the complete opposite of nerdy, smart, and sensitive little Hope. Needless to say, for their mutual friend to be trying to hook them up just a few years later, well it all seemed humorous, especially because sceptical Hope was bewildered that her friend's plan actually worked. The last twist in the puzzle was the fact that this mutual friend was Victor's girlfriend at this party years prior, and Hope made a point that her best friend was dating "an asshole". Here was Hope, falling head over heels for this punk of a boy she'd disliked so much, and part of her hesitation was the person sitting next to her through all this was Victor's ex-girlfriend, but now one of his best friends. Somehow, this all worked. They all became best friends, striding through the jealousy and tension, and growing up with love and gratitude.

It was no love at first sight, but Hope couldn't help but feel butterflies at the sight of him after their first night of hitting it off. She had a crush, like a bubbled-over, crazy, wonderful crush. How hope yearned for those butterflies at this very moment, as she reminded herself not to get overly intrigued by the glitz and glamour of her flashbacks. This was a different feeling of crush now, not the crazy-wonderful, but the crazy-crunch-bang, nothing left to salvage type of crush. Those happy times were long-gone. The bruise on her arm leaped out at her again, and she spent a few seconds staring at it, like if she stared long enough, it would just disappear, along with the devastation and drama, but instead it just proved to her that there were several not-so-pretty times for her and Victor too.

All the self-confidence that Victor had helped Hope to establish during the first several months of their relationship and the invigorating sense of self-worth he had helped her to find, well, instantaneously, that could be torn right back down, boom boom boom. Consequently, every time Victor did something to hurt Hope, whether he meant to or not, whether he realised the cost of his actions or not, he was breaking her spirit down, inch by inch. Meaningless intoxicated sex with various women, that was the start, followed by disconnection, the period where Victor actually allowed himself to stop loving Hope. He numbed himself with his consumption of alcohol, thus not feeling the pain anymore, leaving Hope to feel like she meant nothing to him, lost, empty and alone. Sadly, in a drunken slur, Victor had babbled out those words, admitting he did not feel in love with Hope anymore.

Just as clear as the wonderful memories, Hope also retained mental images of horrendous times, times which she would rather forget, or erase. The best example, besides last night, would probably be the first time Victor ever admitted to being unfaithful. The immediate reaction was like a severe burn, and the intensity of the flames of a red-hot fire. The pain was brutally unavoidable, like a slap in the face, and the heat was a shock to the system, that left Hope lost for words. She couldn't speak, or the smoke of the fire would choke her.

She wanted to slap the stupid smirk off his face, as he was telling her what happened, but then his smirk became a melt-down of tears and sorrow, and loving terms of endearment, including hundreds of apologies and him begging her for another chance. The scars were hideous and everlasting. The feelings were very surreal, like a dream, but not the type of dream you want to chase by falling back asleep after the alarm clock interrupts your precious slumber. What made it easier was his stupid, bullshit promises, the words that Hope believed at the time, when he said, "Never again".

Hope was in denial, a rush of disbelief, then she suddenly drowned in anger, ready to kill him for being so stupid. She grieved the perfectness they had, and felt like this was undo-able damage. The betrayal she was experiencing was tying hundreds of large knots in her stomach, leaving a nauseating weakness within. She felt violated, she felt disgust, she felt like she was breaking. A lump was welling up in her throat. She had pushed back the tears in the moment, because the safety she had felt in Victor was vanished. She did not want to bear her feelings to him. She could not attest to him that he had the power to crush her like a little bug. Instead she would play it cool, but he could see right through her. At that moment, a part of Victor was shattered too. He did love Hope, it was never phoney or untruthful, he had just made a very big mistake. Unfortunately this mistake was the beginning of a very slippery slope. He was sorry, he really did not want to be that guy. He should have learned his lesson, but instead he blamed drinking, and this would not be his last offence.

Perhaps Victor felt so bad about himself, that maybe he tried drinking away the pain and guilt, only creating more trouble. Cycles, cycles, everywhere. That did not excuse him, but it may have been his legitimate reasoning. Victor had become his own worst nightmare, and an enemy to himself, and from there, it just continued like a bullet wound gushing with blood. Several deceptions were still to come, and a predictable pattern of events followed, but somehow Hope believed in the sweetness of the aftermath, always believing that his selfish ways were done. She hoped his guilt would make him into a better boyfriend, because he would feel so bad that he would go out of his way to be better. In all honestly, Victor also thought each act of infidelity was his last, for each time he saw the despair in Hope's eyes, he broke himself a little more, but he also was shutting himself down more and more because he would always turn back to a bottle to ease his guilt. Shame on him for committing the crimes, shame on her for being an accomplice. She should have walked away.

Meanwhile, Hope knew the woman . . . or girl . . . or tramp . . . or whatever you want to call the female that he had sexually gratified in the midst of a good intoxication session at its' highest. She could kill them both. She remembered thinking how heartless some people are, and how thoughtless. Some people do not think of the consequences of their actions, but how could they, when their minds are so drenched in booze and stupidity? This would be the beginning of Hope's hatred towards alcohol. It would take Hope a few more years to realise that being drunk is really not a good enough excuse for infidelity. Before she could really understand that fact, she would have to live the life of an alcoholic's wife, but only in a common-law fashion, because Victor swore he would never get married, another wedging factor that might play a role in the distance of Hope and Victor over-time.

Marriage ruins things as far as Victor was concerned. That was the vision of marriage that was etched into his mind from a very young age. For Hope, that was her dream, one of the visions she always had for herself, the big picture in life; to get married and have a family. That would define her, and that was all she ever wanted. In her opinion, the only factor that would ruin things for them, was his drinking. To Hope, marriage was still a beautiful thing, and a proper way of life for people when they fall in love. Nobody could take that dream away from her, whether it ever happened or not, Hope would never believe Victor's negative rants.

Hope would watch romantic movies and bawl her eyes out, always fantasizing that someday that would be her, but always fearing that she may never find true love. She would go to weddings and feel captivated by the love, even when she barely knew the couple. The atmosphere of weddings brought her joy, and made her want to reach for the stars. She would watch the bride walk down the aisle, looking like a princess and think how amazing it would feel to find someone who wanted to spend the rest of his life with her, who was that in love with her. She wanted one day to feel like a princess. She would look at the groom and be so delighted that a man could melt into mush for one day, to give his bride her perfect day. She loved when you could see the love in the groom's eyes, sometimes even a hint of tear, as he would watch his beauty step towards their future. She hated the male ego of being too cool for love that some man seemed to portray. Hope couldn't understand why anyone would want to avoid such a perfectly, beautiful, magical day. She didn't think Victor felt too cool for marriage, he was just scared and turned off by it, and who could blame him if they lived in his shoes?

In the midst of her flashbacks, Hope's reflections took her back to another moment where she felt Victor's love was stronger than steal, but as soft as wool. She was only about seventeen, and they had probably been together about a year. A night at the movies took a turn for disaster, winding her up in the hospital, after what doctors diagnosed as probably a seizure. Victor had watched her do the funky chicken, flopping and twitching in a state of unconsciousness, which had given him a sick worried fear of losing her.

Hope would spend the next few nights in the hospital undergoing several tests, and she remembered being very scared. "What if something is deathly wrong with me", she thought. Her life was so wonderful, and she had so much to live for, so of course that is when something bad would happen, thus being why she feared the worst. Everyday her fears and feelings of entrapment were eased for awhile as a special someone was by her side, that special someone being Victor of course. One of those evenings, he laid beside her in the squishy hospital bed, and resting his head on her shoulder, he told her not to be scared. He wanted to spend the night just so she wouldn't feel so alone. He was also scared, but didn't not want her to know that. He wished he could make everything ok again for her. As she stared into his eyes, tears welled in her own, for she could see and feel the love gushing out of them, seeping through his veins and bringing a calming sense of peace to the room. They got lost in each others stares, like the whole world was right there between them and nothing else mattered in that second.

As Victor held Hope's hand, she felt like she could beat the odds of whatever was wrong. With his help, she could conquer the world, and overcome anything. Their love was so enticingly compelling. Hope had not showered for the past three days, and the odours of her sweat were probably scarier than any weapon. She had no make-up on, her hair was matted looking, like a dirty old dog, and she felt like a big grease ball. Of course, her sexy hospital negligee was the icing on the cake. Her rawest vulnerabilities were exposed, and here was the man of her dreams, still practically drooling over her, at one of her weakest states.

Victor had unhinged her inhibitions, and she felt accepted, and even special. Unlike any other relationship she had been in, Hope could be herself, right down to the nitty gritty. Her inner beauty finally mattered. Now that is true love. Gross, raw, but real—and true. Love isn't about appearance, make-up, and pretty clothes, instead it is about the under layers, and this was a beautiful example, or not so beautiful if you looked at poor Hope. Love is the person standing by your side when times get tough.

Hope adored Victor one hundred and fifty percent for his true wonderfulness, until the day that he was kidnapped by the luscious brew of beer, robbed right out from under her. She would do almost anything to have him back, and to get back those moments. With a beaming grin on her face, Hope was suddenly slammed back to reality like a blow to the head. "How?" "How in the hell did we get from that moment to this in the blink of an eye?" Now Victor would probably leave her in the hospital to rot, let alone lay in her stink. "Where did the love go?" Hope wondered. It didn't make sense. How did this man who was once waiting on her hand and foot, ready to kiss her feet and slave to her, now become the enemy, the opposition, ready to knock her flat on her face? "How?" No matter how many times she repeated that word, and that question, she didn't have an answer.

# CHAPTER NINE

NOTHER UNFORGETTABLE DAY FULL of beauty and pride for Hope was her high school graduation. She received several awards and scholarships, and had achieved one of the top grades in the class. She wore a white dress with red print flowers dazzled all around. Hope was a ball-room beauty, who had never felt prettier until that day. She could see how proud her parents were, and she was soaking in all the wonders of the day, knowing she had worked hard and earned every bit of what she felt. What made the whole experience more remarkable was her escort, the man who stood by her side, watching her make her mark on the world, one of the many steps of greatness in his eyes. As they danced, early into the evening, he pulled her in closely and whispered into her ear,

`I'm so proud of you, and you look beautiful`.

A single tear rolled out of Victor's gorgeous eye, and as he quickly composed himself, while butterflies danced around inside Hope. He looked so incredibly handsome as he spoke from his heart, words of true love. Those words stuck with Hope forever, the teardrop zoomed-in in her imagination, and made that day amazing. In fact, during some of her lonely, long University days, she would use that memory to smile and ease her way through a difficult moment. Speaking of zooming, just as fast as she could get lost in these great times gone by, her mind could skip back to present, to the opposite feeling of horror. Her life just felt like a big conspiracy now, a tug of war, between good and evil.

Enemies. That was what they had become to each other. When things first started falling apart, she remembered thinking they had become roommates, but not close friendly ones. They existed together, that was about the extent of them now. They weren't lovers, they weren't friends, they didn't communicate anymore, unless you call cursing and swearing and calling each other childish or obscene names communication, and the respect was gone right out the window. No compassion, no attraction, no trust, no loyalty, no desire, no more excitement, no more butterflies, no more happiness. Those marvels were dead and buried. Only negativity presided there now. They brought out the worst in each other. At this moment, despite the fond memories, Hope felt like giving up. There was absolutely nothing left. It was too late to ever find her way back to those good times.

Hope's mind drifted next to her university days again, this time to a friend of hers who had opened up to her about her abusive relationship with her boyfriend. This couple were constantly fighting, and it often got physical and violent. One night, in a drunken rage, he came home and woke her up by throwing her out of the bed. This girl hadn't even instigated him, but of course she fought back, and ended up plummeting down the stairs. She had broken ribs, and wound up in the hospital, and he landed himself in prison obviously.

Hope remembered feeling very sympathetic towards the girl, feeling like she was in the middle of a novel, as she told her story, but thinking that nothing like that could ever happen to her. She would never in a million years allow herself to fall victim to such stupidity and drama. "How did people get themselves into these situations?", she had wondered, as she took pity on the girl next to her. Now Hope distinctly understood, and her sympathy had become empathetic compassion, for she was equally as weak. Now she was the girl who had inadvertently gotten caught in a stupid, dramatic situation. These things don't just happen in books and movies. They sneak up on the best of people.

At the time when this girl was revealing herself to Hope, Hope had compared Victor to this scumbag the girl called her boyfriend, feeling lucky to have someone who was so decent and respectful of women. There was no way in hell Victor could ever treat her like that, not only because of his strong love for her, but also because that wasn't him. That was not in his nature, and he was not a violent man in any sense. She never imagined that he had the potential to become violent, and that she of all people would be the target for which his violence would erupt upon, and the trigger to his dark side.

Victor had gone from a slight ass, to a full-out asshole, the vulgar words that popped into Hope's head when she thought of him now. He had flicked a switch to turn off all emotion. Alcohol helped to lessen the pain, and make everything feel fine. Hope, on the other hand, felt every little poke and prod, and every word he muttered. She felt it all, immensely, but her mind was shutting down. Her thoughts weren't always rational, but she followed her heart . . . her poor foolish heart. She floated through the bad times with optimism, but the optimistic side of her was on its last leg. Scepticism and discouragement had come out ahead now.

Hope used to be one of the world's most positive people, but funny how things change. Well, actually, not funny, very sad in fact. Hope felt drained and exhausted, tired of pretending, tired of dreaming, tired of waiting, tired of being so naive and dumb. Nothing and nobody were worth these feelings. Her poor moronic heart was at its wits end. She, as a person, could not tolerate anymore, but it scared the hell out of her to think of what the future had in store for her now, without the love of her life by her side for support and love. Could she really pack up, and pick up, without Victor, and with only the memories left of him and her. She wasn't alone in that decision anymore, which made it even more difficult.

She knew, if absolutely necessary, a last resort, she could survive without Victor, with the love of her little girl, whom she was thankful to have, more than ever now. Quite frankly, Hope and Victor had not been together for some time, but neither of them was openly admitting the collapse yet. Tiny threads that Hope was clinging to was all that they had left. "Where," thought Hope, "where is the rewind button on life?" "Love isn't supposed to feel this way", she noted out loud. Talking to herself was becoming a norm.

Victor was so bitterly cold, yet his words burned like red-hot flames in an uninviting tone. He was so insensitive when he spoke, his words like daggers, piercing deep into the flesh of her heart and soul. Victor was so argumentative, and though he swore he didn't cause the fights, he really had become confrontational. He was loud-mouthed, rude, and aggressive, both with words and actions. Victor would always slam the door, and take off when an argument spiralled. He felt this best to avoid a fight, but Hope just thought he was a coward. Hope hated when he walked away, heightening her anger. He may come back cooled off, and she would be more worked up then when he'd left. So petty, but so heated. The tense silence would last twenty minutes tops while Hope sat stewing, then she boiled over, and a massacre would erupt each time. Never a happy ending, rehash the past, blame and point, grumble and grumble, and nobody heard the other's points without feeling offended and a need to defend. Mostly, nobody heard the others point at all. Always a battlefield, but never a centre for healing or any common ground. They needed a mediator. No healing, no fixing, just deeper and deeper in a hole of grit and grime.

Just as hatred was infusing its' way into Hope's feelings toward Victor again, she jumped back yet again to another time where love conquered. There was another time-frame in Hope's past, marked by tragedy, pain, suffering, and a severe loss in the family. A tiny blue casket would disrupt the nature of what is right, and point in the direction of what is just oh so wrong in this world. A time that allowed Hope to feel the ugly side of the world, and the most difficult time in her life up to that point would reintegrate its way back into the picture. Despite the grief, Hope had such a strong, huge rock to lean on at the time, a shoulder to cry on, soaked in her tears, and someone who was equally as touched by the mourning. He had become such a piece of the family, that he felt the loss alongside Hope, when her older sister gave birth to her baby boy prematurely. He was given about ten hours of life and a chance to make his imprint, but then he left just as quickly as he came in. Hope had Victor, who was a god-sent at the time. Life works in mysterious ways, and Hope just could not find an answer in why this had happened, and this was one episode in her life that she would never be able to reason with.

Hope had summarized her emotion through a poem shortly after the tragedy, one which she entered into her grade 12 Poetry Portfolio for her high school English Project, which left her teacher and several classmates speechless. That was always part of Hope's healing or at least a way to deal when emotions got to be too much. She loved to write. Whether it be poetry, short stories, a diary, a letter, or just a page, writing was her sanctuary. Her heart would escape onto paper. She entitled this poem, "Heartache" —

*Heartache is like a headache. Only no medicine can cure. Only time can heal.*

*And some just never goes away. My most recent heartache, was the loss . . . of a precious baby boy.*

*Excitement filled my heart. To know my sister was pregnant. But he came too early. His little lungs just didn't have the strength. God had another plan for him . . .*

*The hardest time in my life so far. A tiny blue casket. A mother's loving words of goodbye. A father carrying away his baby boy. LULLABIES.*

*The hurt, the grief, the tears. I'll never see my first nephew. My sister will never watch her first child grow. He'll never play catch with his daddy. His big sister will never get to read to him. He'll never be spoiled by his grandparents, Aunts, Or his Uncle. All I saw were pictures. Tiny enough to fit into the palm of a hand. But his effect was huge. The heartache will get easier. But we'll never forget*

*Our Little Angel, Matthew!*

When her sister went into labour, rushed circumstances didn't allow Hope to join her parents on their trip into the city to be with their older daughter, nor did their mother really want Hope to be there, knowing the risk involved. Hope's mother knew that Hope was in good hands, as she'd been out at Victor's family farm for the weekend, when this occurred. Hope wanted so badly to be with her sister and her parents, but during her fall, who better to catch her than Victor, considering her family was preoccupied, understandably. His family was her support system, during her hellish year. Her family's sadness created an ever greater strength for Hope and Victor. That year may have cemented them, time after time, whenever Victor could define his love through his acts of kindness and support. His family, and especially him, made that night more bearable for poor frail little Hope.

After hearing the news from her mom by phone, Hope ran to the bathroom in disbelief, unable to breath, but not wanting to cave in front of Victor and his father. She needed a moment to herself to fall apart and let herself go. She was so crushed, as the thrill of aunty-hood was ripped from beneath her, not to mention, her poor sister. Hope couldn't even imagine the loss her sister must be enduring, and sympathy wasn't a strong enough word. She was devastated for her sister, her brother-in-law, her parents, and the rest of the family, who would all suffer the loss. Her heart drowned, as tears welled up from the root of her, and gushed like rain. Victor's dad knocked, and when Hope didn't answer, he walked in to find her huddled up on the floor, weeping profusely. He picked her up, and gave her the biggest, bear hug, that was such a comfort. His arms surrounding her also caused her to break down even more. Hope remembered feeling a fatherliness about him. Like a second dad. In her books, he was always there, when it really and truly mattered. Both of these men, Victor and his dad, had capabilities to be the softest loving men on earth, and yet, they also had the abilities to be the most cruel and senseless men she knew. They were puzzling men, but their mysteriousness pulled Hope in. She would never forget their moments of greatness. Never.

Victor had wished that he could delete Hope's heartache, and bring back the joy she had felt when she discovered her sister's pregnancy. He remembered how excitement would always bleed off of Hope, such heartiness always sprung from her during times of greatness, but when she fell, she really tumbled . . . down, down, down. She was so delicate. She wasn't just falling, but falling apart, and this was one her darkest hours, ever. Victor could not stand seeing her like that. The poor girl had such misery in her eyes, and just when she'd feel slight ease, tears would find their way yet again to her burning eyes, all the while such a blankness stood where her smile usually sat, and such hate for the higher power, in charge of this nonsense was running through Hope. Victor's love for her in this moment, was outrageous, and beyond belief.

# CHAPTER TEN

OPE CONTINUED TO DRIFT on, to another night of agony this time. Her and Victor had been out at a social, together, but not really together. They no longer acted like a couple, and nobody would know they were once in love, just by the distance that stormed off them. Even people who knew them as a couple could probably read the distance without much doubt anymore. Victor was so dysfunctionally drunk out of his mind, staggering and looking like a complete idiot in Hope's eyes, and in the eyes of anyone else who wasn't equally inebriated. Hope allowed herself to escape, by getting lost in the love of another couple.

A young pregnant lady had caught Hope's attention. She loved the idea and everything that trailed along with pregnancy, something about the entity of pregnancy called out to her, and she couldn't help but see the glow of this beautiful woman, and the glow between her and the man she was with. So happy. Hope was able to find a smile just by watching these lovebirds. "If love like that never lasts, why do we bother at all", questioned Hope. A bitter sweet feeling reigned over Hope, and as she glanced back at the love of her life, who didn't know whether he was coming or going, she felt confusion for where she should go with the rest of her life. Did this couple stand a better chance at love then she had? Hope knew that her unhappiness was no longer concealed, and everyone in the room probably knew that her and Victor were falling apart and their relationship was only a matter of time now.

Hope suddenly caught a glimpse of Victor at his flirtatious high, being a complete and ignorant pig to another woman, right in front of her. He couldn't have been more inappropriate if they got naked in front of Hope at that very second. When she confronted him, just minutes later, when the women was out of sight, he just swore at her. He didn't try to lie anymore, he didn't try to make excuses or cover anything up. Now he had no qualms about what he did, what she saw, or how she felt. He was a complete heartless jerk. A slap in the face, not literally, but just the same. Hope was shocked that women actually fell for Victor's drunk seduction, but when she saw the bimbos he chased, perhaps it was an obvious connection. Luckily, this particular woman would not give Victor the satisfaction or time of day.

Victor told Hope that night that she could leave, and that he wouldn't care, and that he would be happy to get her off his back. He spat the words at her, with such loathing, and that look of hatred in his eye yet again frightened Hope. He did this in front of several people, without any concern. Everyone minded their own business, and nobody spoke a word to Hope. Victor spoke to Hope this way now, and she was so accustomed to hearing these words from him, that they barely had an effect. This night however, she did feel the throbbing, quite fiercely, with every fibre of her being. She hated him that night. He seemed like a total stranger to her, and the Victor she loved was dead.

Hope should have left him right then, and let him see how much his words impacted her, and the consequences of his stupidity. She was just as foolish, pretending it never happened. He was killing her inside, and that night particularly, she wanted to cry, but couldn't, at least not in front of everyone. She went home and pitied herself, wondering what steps to take next. Pity was stronger than wit. Usually she calmed her nerves with some sleep, and woke up less ready to end things, and more willing to make amends.

Most socials or events that Hope would have liked to attend were write-offs to her now. Her own social life was basically non-existent. First of all, if they did both go somewhere, she did not want to witness Victor carrying on like a fool, while he put his moves on other women, or tried picking a fight with some random guy. The sad truth was that Hope expected this stupid behaviour from Victor, and did nothing to stop it anymore, because she felt she had no say. Instead she just avoided seeing it for herself.

Why was she still there? That was what most sane people would ask. Especially considering, Hope was embarrassed and ashamed of Victor these days. It was not like they ever stayed together, like a couple or anything, on outings. The concept of being girlfriend and boyfriend, partners, parents, or anything resembling a relationship between adults was missing between these two, and believing they were ever a pair was impossible.

Secondly, Hope was usually the one stuck at home when Gracie's grandparents were unable to baby-sit, and she often didn't even bother asking anymore. Even when Victor may have been willing to take turns attending something specific that might be important to Hope, by the time his shift came along, he would be so drunk, Hope would be an unfit mother to leave him alone with their daughter. He would have to take the first shift, and that just never seemed to happen. Hope was scared to make plans with friends, because she could not rely on Victor anymore, and never knew when he just wouldn't come back home in time for her to go out.

Victor always said he didn't mind, and she deserved a social life too, but he never lived up to his words. Somehow, whether it was done on purpose or not, Victor was able to ruin her plans or hinder her from making any, keeping her at home in isolation and solitude. This in turn made Hope resentful and bitchy, just adding fuel to the fire of their problems. Victor thought she whined too much, and really did not sympathize. He was resentful, but not towards Gracie, just towards Hope's attitude.

There was never a chance to resolve any fight because Victor would just pretend it never happened, and tell her to get over it if she tried to return to the situation. She was at her final breaking point, where one must decide. Could she use her last ounce of courage and move along, and leave Victor and this seemingly unchangeable past behind. That would mean that Hope would have to admit that she had failed, that she did not have the ability to change Victor, that she was not enough for him to quit drinking, and that she wasn't worthy. All these factors were eating away at Hope, and she was seriously on the verge of quitting. Fear was a big part of holding her back.

"For Christ Sake, he quit me along time ago," thought Hope. "Payback is a bitch", flickered in her brain. Hope was trying to strengthen her ego, but she knew that Victor would just keep drinking his life away, whether she left or not. The sad truth was, he didn't care, because he had shut down. He stopped caring about everything and everyone long ago, except for the love he couldn't ignore, his daughter. Hope just wanted to find happiness again, but she was petrified and felt paralyzed. She needed help. No matter what the outcome, or what decisions were made, Hope knew the reality was that her and Gracie were the only sufferers, and Victor wouldn't suffer unless he stopped fermenting his body, which was unlikely.

Victor's harsh words echoed at her, "I don't love you anymore . . . you are nothing but a B*t*H . . . . you make me want to leave . . . . you make me drink . . . . I can't stand being around you . . . naggy . . . whiny . . . good for nothing . . ." These were regular phrases that came directly out of Victor's mouth. Hope had always promised herself never to stoop to the level of calling out hurtful names and vengeful, hate-filled words in such an immature manner, but now she found herself throwing vulgar slogans in the air, and expressing herself the way she had been talked to ordinarily. She felt like she had to fight back or she would be the weaker party, but after the disputes would cool down, she was just left feeling stupid and childish. This was Hope's protective front, and she used these ugly words to hide her fragility. She wanted to set herself on a level of higher standards, the pedestal for the good guy, but in truth, she was starting to hate who she was when they'd fight. This malicious beast would just protrude it's way out of her, and she did not want to continue allowing her identity to become this darker side of herself. She knew she had to stop.

Hope was so frustrated with herself for putting up with this nonsense and playing this foolish game for this long. She was aggravated that she had let things get this far out of control. It was a crazy shambled disaster that was too far gone to undo. Hope was undoubtedly sure that a part of her was evaporated into thin air eternally, and that she could never retrace that best sense of herself. That saddened Hope, because even if her and Victor parted ways and somehow came to terms with raising Gracie separately, and even if they could maintain decency with time, and even if they healed slightly from the break, that piece of Hope had just seen too much ugliness to ever resurface. Gracie would never witness the best side of her mommy, even if Hope wanted her too.

Even if they could recover from this, in whatever form that took, Hope withheld permanent injury. Getting to that comfort point again was also the difficult task Hope didn't know how to tackle, after all she had done the letting go thing in the past, and knew all to well how hard that really is. Maybe some people can just move along, free as a bird, but that wasn't Hope. Hope knew she did not deserve to be spoken to or treated so disgracefully. She also knew that beating Victor down with the same stick he beat her with was only going to leave them both battered and bruised. It was unhealthy for everyone. There was no easy answer, and nothing Hope could choose to do would make sense, not one way or another.

# CHAPTER ELEVEN

OPE ACTUALLY DREADED THE weekends, the days which should be her sanctuary, her relief from a busy week, and some relaxing family time. Those used to be her favorite days, and what she looked forward to all week long. Instead, now those days were lonely, just her and Gracie, and that was the time Victor let loose the most of course. She knew that come Fridays he was not likely to come straight home from work, and when he did, he ate and left again. He avoided her calls, and definitely stretched the truth, lying about where he was, how long he had been there, and of course, about how many drinks he had already consumed. In the earlier days, he tried really hard to make it sound better, but now, Victor really didn't give a damn, and just didn't bother letting Hope in on anything. Sometimes she didn't see him again till Sunday night, sometimes not till Monday. She started running away to her mom's all the time for the entire weekend, using that as a threat to get Victor home, but he didn't care. He was happy to see her leave, out of sight, out of mind, and out of his way.

Hope loved the time at her mom's, and it made her mind forget the chaos back home, but those days and hours would always fly by, and she would have to face that drive home, each time wondering what she would find. Would he be there, would he return, or would the sun go down with her lonely heart? What Hope never realised was that when she wasn't with Victor, on her little escapee get-aways, she felt less stressed, and if she could just have strength to let go completely, she might find happiness again. Nobody should stay in a relationship that is that stressful and leaves no room for any good. Hope was holding on to something that no longer existed, and really, she may have found better had she found the courage to look. Who knows what life might have had to offer beyond these heavy doors.

As a care provider, Hope had learned that one of the top notch ways to manage negative behaviour patterns in children is with redirection. Victor was acting like a child, at least Hope felt as such, so why not treat him like one? Hope started trying to search for excuses throughout the week, seeking out events that Victor shouldn't miss because they were important family events. If there was something more enjoyable to occupy him, maybe he wouldn't want to go partying, drinking, and seeking out that excitement. Hope just wanted his presence to be with her, but she wanted the sober version. She couldn't stand to be around the drunk version. Whatever 'excuse', or plan, what have it, he usually skipped or ended up late anyway, usually causing a fight, leaving Hope upset and not wanting to attend whatever they were to attend. She hated going alone and making excuses for Victor's absence. She hated waiting for him to show up, deep down knowing he wasn't going to at least 85% of the time. She couldn't even be her happy self around her own family anymore.

Hiding the truth was becoming more and more difficult, and Hope was sure that everyone could read her mind and see the true grey and stormy colors of their relationship through her saddened eyes. Hope wanted to crawl into a box and avoid everyone. It was all part of the ugly unhealthy cycle she was spinning around on. Hope should have seen that Victor was one of those children that just doesn't want to be redirected. His behaviour patterns were fairly predicable, but Hope didn't want to see that. He was one of THOSE types alright. She was out of patience for this unruly child.

In the pandemonium of her feelings and of the life she now lived, Hope also blamed her house for some of the unruliness. Yes, her house. Hope was convinced that their new home was haunted, and she really was scared of being alone, at night especially. With a newborn, and a spouse who enjoyed the nightlife and left her stranded and alone, this was much more complicated. This added to her feelings of entrapment, and made the evenings seem even longer when Victor was out on the town, gallivanting the night away while she felt threatened in her own home. She often felt like she was going insane, when she sat back to swallow up her surroundings. She swore that she could hear voices of people talking in their basement, as she laid in bed, fighting to sleep. She would lay awake, listening, trying to be so careful and quiet. Yet part of her wanted to leave the TV or some music on, just so she couldn't hear anything else. One minute she was so sure, then another minute or two would pass, and she would question herself again. Was her mind playing tricks? She felt an eerie sense fluttering over her at times, like someone was watching her. Goosebumps and tears would be unavoidable, and anxiety would leave Hope feeling like she could run away, even in crazy hours of the night.

Even during the day, sometimes she would just feel strange, and downstairs specifically brought goose bumps to her, and she could not bring herself to go down there to do laundry after dark. It came as no surprise to Hope to discover that someone had actually died at the bottom of their basement stairs. A man had fallen, breaking his neck. That was evidence to Hope, only giving her suspicions clarity, but giving her a spine-tingling and eye-watering chills. Hope wondered if that was why they had been sold the house so cheaply.

"They knew", she thought, feeling like she was suckered into something. To know that the lady who had most recently lived in the house previous to them had also just passed away, only added to the idea as far as Hope was concerned. The elderly lady had known Victor's family well, and Victor's mother had grown up with this lady's children, but Hope never had the chance to meet her. She was ill when they had decided to sell the house, but she got worse fast, and ended up in a Care Home, leaving her children to sell faster than planned.

The elderly lady had insisted that they be able to have the house for a deal, because she wanted them to have a good start with a baby on the way, which Hope thought was sweet. It should be peaceful to think this lady may be watching over them, but to Hope, a ghost is a ghost, and there is no peace in a presence like that. The husband had passed away in his bed years prior, in the very room that Hope now slept each night, and Hope was left filled with thoughts of death, dreariness and grief. The walls were filled with stories, she thought, and Hope was not comforted by the stories. They were not warm and fuzzy bedtime stories that you can tell the kids at night. In her gloomy reality, this gloomy scene didn't help.

One of the weirdest, unexplainable experiences Hope ever had, occurred one night when she was searching through pictures on the internet. They were old pictures that belonged to the daughter-in-law of the lady who they had bought the house from, a lady Hope had befriended through the community and her in-laws. These photos contained the old homeowner and her grandchildren, and the first time Hope laid eyes on the elderly lady she never had the chance to meet, her eyes filled with tears. A sense of sadness washed over, and she knew there had to be a connection to that lady and the house at present. Hope had goose bumps again, and had to stop looking at these pictures.

Hope didn't even like Gracie sleeping in her own room. She wanted to protect her little girl, and snuggle her all night, safely, in her arms. To feel uncomfortable in your own home, while raising a baby, is not easy to say the least. The strangeness and discomfort ate at Hope, leaving her feeling more miserable, and wanting to leave. She was losing her marbles, and falling apart. She begged Victor not to leave at night. He just saw it as whining, nagging, and controlling. A stupid excuse to him. He didn't understand.

Getting a dog was a security for Hope, and probably the answer to her prayers. It was as if the spirits were lifted and decided to move on, or perhaps these outer worldly presences were scared of the dog. Was Hope's imagination a little over-active? Did she spend too much time in solitude? Or was her new slobbery, hairy, untrained idiot her new best friend? That dog could annoy her all day long, but when the sun went down, she truly enjoyed the company and comfort she brought. That hound made her feel better than Victor ever did anymore. The security he once brought to Hope was in the past.

# CHAPTER TWELVE

HOPE REMEMBERED THE DAYS where a few tears or even her pouty face could leave Victor grovelling apologetically at her feet eventually. She always had a way of making him feel bad, wanting to fix things. Sometimes they would both be sorry, and turn their arguments into a joke, and that would be that, done like dinner . . . carry on. Victor could never stay mad at her for long, and she was not a grudge holder either, but those days had disappeared into the sunset, and the sun never seemed to rise anymore in their household. Nowadays Victor really couldn't care less when Hope was mad, and he likewise, stayed mad at her more often than not. When they weren't fighting, that was a breakthrough, which would be short-lived. The pout no longer had any effect on Victor, the tears didn't even hit a nerve, in fact her emotion only triggered his in a negative fashion now, quite contrary to the old days. Hope felt so unloved, and so unimportant. She felt like she was at a dead end and stuck, unable to turn around, and unable to move forward. Just stuck! And Hopeless.

During one of their hundred attempts to make amends and really try working things out, Hope and Victor actually agreed to counselling, and she made some calls, seeking out free help. To Hope's surprise, Victor willingly went to the sessions, and actually felt a breakthrough when they sat down and talked with the counsellor, feeling equal, talking without blame and anger. Their first session resulted in both Victor and Hope feeling in love again, mended, and on the road to recovery. However, the truth of the matter was that neither of them was really getting to the heart of the problem. They were wishy-washing their way around the bigger picture, the real issue. Nobody spoke out about Victor's drinking. Hope certainly drew attention to the subject, but like usual, it was downplayed, and the counsellor never got a full view of the issue. She took them as typical youth, and was lead to believe that Victor was merely a social drinker, who ran away in arguments, and used drinking as an escape from fighting and boredom. These analyses were true, but there was so much more to the matter, and bottling up her true feelings left Hope with underlying concern.

Victor might not be fully dependant on alcohol yet. Sure, he could minimize the issue by claiming that he didn't drink every day, but he was heading down that road. For now, he was just parked at the "Stop In and Binge" Hotel Express, where 'the faster you get drunk, the better you feel'. He could cruise on in a daze to "Pass Out and Forget", a little pit stop he frequently made these days. In the morning he could awake to a Continental 'Hangover Special', including Barley Soup du Jour and a Tall glass of last night's special, most likely another beer. He hid his feelings in a bottle, but certainly didn't care how the odd one slipped out, in it's most threatening and unflattering form.

In Victor's eyes, things were much better, with counselling he had felt this revitalization, and somehow came up with the idea of marriage, perhaps seeking a new thrill and need for excitement in his life. Maybe he truly believed that would fix them. Hope loved how it sounded, a glimpse of her dreams coming true, but she still worried about the future, still feeling avoidance with things that should be discussed. Hope did feel on cloud nine when Victor told the counsellor he wanted to get married soon, because things were so much better, and she certainly saw a reconnection between the couple, leaving her to believe they didn't really need her help anymore. It was too rushed, too forced, too played-up, making a mockery of counselling even.

Weeks went by, and they were back at square one, fighting and carrying on. Hope would listen to wedding songs online, and do some research on planning a wedding, and some dreamy ideas danced in her head, but Victor would shrug her off, and she certainly sensed his hesitations again, so one night she approached the topic, in the aftermath of an argument. The timing was terrible, and Victor told her that they couldn't get married because he didn't even know if they would be together in the future. He could have punched her in the stomach, and it would not have hurt as bad. Hope knew what Victor was saying was true, but for some reason, these words left her feeling so brittle and broken. She would never forget that night, laying in bed, trying to muffle her cries, wishing he could see her pain, wishing he would acknowledge her feelings. She felt so out of touch and out of sync with him. They were living in totally different worlds for the umpteenth time.

This was a recent pain, still fresh, and their situation had only gotten worse since that conversation, and that cold night. The nights had only gotten colder, the bitter frigidness leaving a frost bite of permanent burn. So once again, the question stood out, who were they trying to fool by continuing on? For Hope, it was still the good times ringing in her ears, and replaying in her visions. Hope could remember so crystal clear, one of her fondest memories, the first time her and Victor made love. The passion flaming between them was so intense. The heat was so breathtaking it could suffocate them. Nothing else in the world mattered; it was them, in the moment, it was love. It was real, and it was pure, and Hope remembered thinking that nothing could ever come between them. They were unstoppable. The best word that Hope used to describe Victor was beautiful. So kind, so gentle, so compassionate.

As he ever-so gently caressed the small of her back, and ran his fingers slowly up and down her spine, her entire body jolted into ecstasy. The warmth and embracement of his body brushing against her own sent Hope into a euphoric state of electrifying delight. He touched her face in such a tender way that she felt her veins could burst. He passionately drew her into a long and intimate kiss. Her body trembled with anticipation, and her heart was pounding so fast, it could probably have beaten right out of her chest. She loved the skin on skin touch, and he loved her satiny softness, melting their bodies into one.

Heaven itself could not feel more Heavenly than the atmosphere surrounding Hope and Victor in their perfect paradise. He had a gift, in Hope's eyes, and she was so excited to unwrap every little trinket within. At her young age, what Hope was doing at that very moment should be considered morally wrong, and yet it felt oh-so-blissfully right. As far as she was concerned, she was committing the most glorifying sin of her life. The union between Hope and Victor had been built up right from the start, day by day, so naturally, so easily, so meant to be, and this was only amplifying and strengthening that bond. This was only completing the package, and there was absolutely no denying now, they belonged together.

They had times where the joys Hope experienced were some of the best times in her life. She felt like Victor opened up her life to opportunities she would have missed if not for him. He made her plain-Jane existence feel elaborate and poised. He taught her about herself and gave her confidence in herself. He was her prince charming.

Hope was always a happy person, but shy, and definitely lacked self-confidence. She always compared herself to the pretty girls, but now Victor was making her feel like a pretty girl. Sometimes she got so lost in a moment, and felt like the prettiest girl alive, thanks to his words, his actions, and the charm he carried. He was very attractive. Deliciously appealing. A catch. And here she was, stealing his heart and it all seemed too good to be true.

That first adventure of making love was unforgettable, no complaints, unlike some teens who engage in meaningless first time sex adventures just to get the deed done. Hope knew Victor was not a virgin when he slept with her, and she was accepting of that. He had been in love before, and yes, he was one step ahead, but that didn't matter to Hope. It had only been one other girl, at that time. She was quite willing to let bygones be bygones, and had no doubts that Victor had no feelings left for this past love. He was so honest about her. Likewise, Hope shared her past heartaches, and all the gushy details about her history.

Unfortunately, her perfect love scene would be contaminated by other pornographic scenes that would invent themselves in her head later on. Victor's unfaithful quandaries later engraved themselves, like hellish hallucinations, just randomly popping up, even in good times. Victor's naked body, which was supposed to be hers, laying next to other naked, faceless bodies would clearly role play in her brain repetitively. What was worse was when those naked women had faces, faces of women she knew, and that would really debilitate her. She was traumatized by his bashes, and all her dignity evaporated. How can a woman hang on to her own self-worth when she has to compete for the man she loves? Love shouldn't be a competition, but Hope didn't know how to let go. She soon realised her weaknesses and learned she was not bullet-proof.

# CHAPTER THIRTEEN

EERING BACK TO PRESENT day, later that afternoon, Hope flounced down the stairs to the laundry room. As she threw a tiny t-shirt into the washing machine, a beam of happiness flashed through her. She couldn't believe how small that shirt was, and yet, on the other hand, she couldn't get over how quickly her daughter was growing. Hope was frightened by the phrase, "Time flies", as it shot through her mind. Adding Victor's shirt to the dirty load gave Hope a strange urge to snuggle it, as if the shirt was a little piece of him. A soft piece of him. A piece of him she could still cling to, however, the shirt was soiled, symbolizing Victor to a tee. She rubbed her face into the shirt, and drew in a scent of him. He had a charming fragrance, which had always comforted Hope. His smell was as intriguing as ever. "If only he still intrigued me, like this", thought Hope.

An ominous sensation sprang up throughout her, as she picked up one her favourite items next. She used to wear this hoodie sweatshirt all the time, though it was actually Victor's. It left her feeling sexy and rugged, feelings she never wore anymore. She noticed a stain on the sleeve, and although it didn't really matter, she couldn't help but feel disappointment, only for the commonness of Victor and the sweater. He too was stained, dirty, and perhaps irreversibly damaged. As the water filled up in the washing machine, a single salty tear joined in off of Hope's face. Ironically her tear would be dancing around with Victor's dirty laundry, helping to cleanse them. She, however, could not be cleansed, and Victor certainly didn't help to try, nor could he be cleansed as far as Hope was concerned. As she resisted the welling of more tears, collecting herself and keeping composure, she sauntered back up the stairs.

Hope's body was taking charge for the day. She heated a bowl of baby food for Gracie's dinner, and realised the day had managed to get away on her, surprisingly enough. She hadn't noticed what she was doing, but she had to keep going. Gracie needed her mommy, and she couldn't just stop. Routine and habit were helping her along, as time carried on, luckily for her. She would probably just have to take things day at a time, because that was really her only option at this point. Survival was essential, but it seemed impossible.

A simple glimpse around the room, the sight of the clutter of toys, a pair of tiny shoes on the mat by the front door, the little pyjama set hanging up, a cute pink sippy cup on the kitchen table, along with a trail of cheerio crumbs . . . all the traces of a child marked around the house. Sometimes that little girl could create quite a mess in just a short time, but her cuteness made it excusable, and those little messes, those little objects, belonging to her little gem, all brought a smile to Hope's face. She loved every little trinket, every article of clothing, and every mess that were her daughter's works of art. Thousands of dollars in jewellery, clothing, and all the riches in the world, would mean nothing, if they replaced these luxuries. Anything that had a connection to her daughter, was absolutely, positively, Priceless. She once felt the same way for Victor, and now she was unsure . . .

Hope was not completely blameless when it came to being unfaithful. She had gone years being the complete and total victim, who would never in a million years return the pain, but unfortunately with time, she did the exact same thing to Victor. It wasn't that she did it purposely to spite him, but rather just by letting herself get caught up in attraction. This was before her days of being pregnant and before the days of becoming a mom. Hope was probably one of the most honest people in the world, well second to her mother that is, but close behind. She definitely had a conscience that didn't leave her side. She was always a loyal friend and put others before herself, so she would not be someone at the top of the list when accusing people of cheating or any moral wrong-doing.

She did not blame the fact that Victor had done it to her, because sadly, and strangely enough, this affair happened when things between Hope and Victor were going well. She found herself feeling dragged in by a friend, into some very dangerously murky waters of seduction. They were just acquaintances through work, who quickly became friends, and this was just on the brink of Hope's new persona of feeling confident in herself again. Apparently she had sex appeal magnifying off of her, and this OTHER man's words were kind and enticing.

Hope and Victor had gone through a messy over-dramatic break-up months earlier, soon mending things, but being apart just long enough for Hope to explore single life and realise that if she let herself, she could be a real man-magnet. She was trying to prove that she didn't need Victor, but she was not fooling anyone. It was all a diversion, just looking for the rebound guy to fill the empty shoes next to her. Even during these stupid break-ups, she never actually had sex with another man, as something always held her back. Hope retrieved enough self-respect to leave that private and special. Circumstances and things guys said gave Hope a boost though, and she felt that Victor didn't have to be her only option, and she was not going to settle, unless he was willing to make some changes and work to keep her. For the first time in her life, she realised she deserved good things. Her and Victor recovered, and Hope felt a new sense of self-love and just wanted to be her best self. She wasn't a little girl any more, and the ugly duckling she once had been had started to feel much more like a beautiful swan.

With that being said, Hope was open to feeling pretty, and found herself in a dressier wardrobe and just giving off striking, more sophisticated vibes. Her new look apparently was appealing and really caught the eye of this friend, who soon began flirting with her, innocently enough, or so Hope thought. She tried to casually brush him off at first, but soon found herself attracted to him as well. As friends, it was more than her looks that drew this young man in, as he found himself falling for Hope's inner beauties as well. He made no qualms in telling her that he had a huge crush on her, and would eventually reveal that he was falling in love with her.

Hope had not laid a hand on him, nor had they shared any form whatsoever of physical intimacy at that point. Perhaps Hope was naive, but she was flattered by the attention, and had no intention on letting anything become of this, which she thought she made clear to this young man. She also didn't want to be a bitch, and totally end the friendship. Another man was so genuinely attracted to her, and he was starting to make it more and more clear. Not so purposely, Hope definitely did some flirting back, and she would later realise that she was digging herself into a hole, a hole that she would have trouble getting back out of.

Her and Victor were very much still together, and here she was feeling attracted to another man. She was ashamed, but a little piece of her liked the feeling of the danger, like a rush that a robber gets after a great heist. She had always been so good, so honest, and this was so out-of-character, but the truth was that after being with someone for a few years, sometimes the sparks start to fade, and therefore when sparks are being lit by a different match, so be it, a spark is a spark. Add some fuel to the fire, and it was burning out of control. Hope knew how wrong that sounded, yet she was young and foolish.

Quite frankly, despite the wrongness of the situation that Hope allowed herself to be involved in, it could have gotten much more wrong. This never became a full-out sexual affair, but it was still cheating, only more as an emotional affair. Hope's conscience still had a voice, and Hope still listened, despite the arousal of the moment. They shared a steamy lip-locking, tongue tangled experience, but Hope stopped it. That was as far as it got. She still had morals and this just felt out of her realm. She made him leave, which of course he tried to argue, but she stood her ground. She knew that even though she had enjoyed that thirty seconds of shame in the moment, now she would have to live with the guilt, forever. Victor definitely popped into her head, as all this was going on.

Would she ever be able to tell Victor? Would he figure it out? It would eat at for months to come before Victor would ever start asking questions. Finally one day, the weight was becoming to much to bear, so she lifted it off her shoulders, but Victor was left the same wounded sort of wreck she had been so many times before. He was angry, and bitter, and broken too. The shoe was on the other foot this time, she was the one inflicting the pain, and it certainly didn't feel any better than being the one torn apart inside. Hope just wanted to undo everything. She wanted to start over with Victor. She wanted to venture back to the days of pure joy. Now at least she could relate to all Victor's past faults. They were both responsible for the damage, and now they had to decide together whether to try to patch it all back together.

Could Victor forgive her, as she had forgiven him so many times in the past? He certainly didn't like being on this end of the spectrum. He too, could now relate more to the true damage he had caused Hope, and he took an oath within himself that he would never again hurt his poor beloved Hope like that. They both wanted to give their love another chance and learn from all their mistakes. "Never again," Victor stated out loud in an empty room that night.

It took a taste of his own bad medicine for Victor to really learn a lesson. The rest of their troubles were far from over though, just as Hope thought it was all going to be ok, and they would rebuild their trust day at a time . . . they fell down a slippery slope, she got pregnant, with Gracie, and she thought they would pull through that, but Victor wasn't making parenthood easy this day and age. Their situation was so beyond complicated, especially for two people so young and so new to adulthood and parenting.

Hope and Victor had fallen into a deep, dark hole. They had forgotten how happy life can make people feel. They had developed a routine, constantly thriving off the other's misery, waiting to take their next lunge at the other. The threat of the year was "I'm leaving you", tossed around so nonchalantly, so often, the effectiveness was dead, and both parties were equally as prone to make the threat. Their behaviours had fallen so off course, so out of nature and out of context, so unlike who they used to be, and their logical thinking patterns were shut down.

Hope could smell the stale, outdated stench of love gone bad, feeling very misinformed. Love is not supposed to have an expiration date. She felt like she was wilting away inside this hole, and nobody realised how deep down she was. She felt so small, so insignificant, in a big old harsh and wicked world. Gasping for breath. She would take a million cavities, or a gigantic and blinding migraine, or even a broken bone; those would hurt less than her heart ached at that second.

Now the man that had swept her so magically off her feet, had been slow-roasting her poor heart for the past several months. Last night he must have decided that he was ready to eat his delicacy, because he took her slightly burnt heart, which had once been so tender, and he threw it into an open-flamed pit, nicely char-broiled, not to a delicious style, but rather to a state of crisp ruin. She was cooked and done. Every part of her being was stinging with pain, like a bad reaction to poison ivy, just itching to feel some type of relief from the pain of being who she was. If only a cool bath, some cream, and a cold compress could cure this sting.

# CHAPTER FOURTEEN

NOTHER MEMORY THAT STUCK out like a sore thumb for Hope was the night when Victor damn near gave her a heart-attack, with a phone call from the police at two o'clock in the morning. When the phone rings at this time of night, anyone knows that it cannot be good news, and sure enough her heart sank when she heard, "Hope, this is 'officer whatever-his-name-was', we have a Victor Grant here, who we picked up for impaired driving" . . . could she be dreaming . . . PLEASE?!? The first assumption Hope had was an accident, something horrible had happened, when she heard, "officer", the sick sadness was taken over by disgust at the rest of the officer's words.

Hope didn't hear the rest of what the officer babbled on about, because she could not grasp on to the concept of Victor being in a police station, let alone, while she was pregnant, at home, sleeping. She had to go to work in the morning, despite being sick lately, and Victor of course would not have considered that when deciding to be an idiot. Hope, unlike Victor, was really trying to be grown up, and responsible in this situation, preparing for the life that was coming. She was in utter disbelief, even though she really shouldn't of been, considering Victor's drinking ways, but at this time, Hope was still in partial denial to the fact that Victor really did have a serious problem. Her denial was only stemmed from his denial, because every time Hope tried to discuss the issue, Victor would get defensive and push her off. Now she couldn't stomach the idea of him losing his licence. He was a criminal. This should not be taken lightly.

To her, this just seemed unbearably wrong. As the initial shock toned a bit, Hope remembered after a pause, some deep sighs, and choking back tears, and she finally got the words out, "But he is a truck driver". As she said the words, she realised the seriousness of the statement.

The officer just calmly responded, "So, we've been told dear, but we need you to come pick him up, if possible, otherwise he will be spending the night, which we really would rather not do." Hope was beyond upset, in a state of shock, literally speechless. He could have been killed, could have killed someone else, and Hope knew this was not his first time drinking and driving, but certainly was the first time he had been caught. She was so appalled that she, the pregnant lady, in her very pregnant state, was being asked to venture out into a cold, snowy, icy, possibly treacherous highway, at a stupid time of night, to pick up an immature low-life who knocked her up and couldn't even care for himself, let alone his future child or pregnant girlfriend. She hated driving at the best of times, and at this very minute she was tired and groggy, considering she had only been asleep a few hours, and for normal people it was the middle of the night. "Normal people sleep, they don't go out cruising after too many god-damn drinks", thought Hope, wanting to scream at the top of her lungs. This was just ridiculous.

Hope wanted to leave him there, to punish him, to torture him, to make him think a little more. Maybe he would be so ashamed to wake up in the drunk tank of a jail that he would finally slow down, or better yet, quit with the drinking. She certainly did not want to look at him right now, and she could have slapped him. Hope was outright pissed off, and whether Victor liked it or not, Hope was calling his mother to come with her to pick him up. She could not care less what mattered to him, or what trouble he was going to be in, because as far as she was concerned, Victor needed to face the music. She was not going to take on the trek by herself either. Besides, if he was scared of anyone right now, it should be her.

It turned out his mom already knew. Victor's cousin was with him, and he had contacted his own mother, who in turn contacted Victor's father, who then called Victor's mother. She was equally distraught, and knew all too well that Hope was in for a long-haul with Victor and his alcoholic tendencies, and that he really was following in his father's footsteps. Victor's mom also blamed herself at times for his drinking habits, due to the life they had lived when Victor was a child, but here she was trying to better her own life, only to constantly be reminded of the damages. She felt sick over the circumstances. Victor hated when his mom told him he was like his father, and Hope also hated hearing it. She did not want to accept that she was destined to be alone, or to live with a drunk. The slope was slippery, and Hope wanted to avoid that slope.

With a baby on the way, Hope had to hope this was Victor's rude awakening, but the sad truth was, Victor really didn't learn a lesson. He learned not to drink and drive, which Hope was thankful for, because she had often worried about him in an accident. Victor was so stubborn, thick-headed, and dense to the idea that something could happen. Victor had thrown a loop in their future, and this would only be the beginning of a messy road ahead. Unemployment, fines, and a new mortgage, well . . . any idiot can do the math on that one and realise it just doesn't add up.

In the days following that mess, Hope would find herself in a spiral of mixed feelings, some days she felt sorry for Victor because she knew he was ashamed, but then other days she didn't want to face him, because she was sick with worry and fear. She felt his shame was not strong enough, considering the trouble he had gotten them into. She was angry with the selfishness of his fun and games, and the effect these choices were now going to have on all of them, including a life on the way. Considering the size of her belly, the future was a huge concern to her, and she wanted to rely on Victor as the man of the house. She wanted to have faith in him to be there to take care of her and their unborn child. He did change his ways slightly, and step up to the plate so to speak, at least for a short while after all this occurred. His changes were enough to ease Hope's mind, and make everyone believe they were going to be ok.

Victor still drank though. Hope knew her happiness would never be complete, unless Victor quit drinking for good. That was what she really wanted, always, and apparently that was way too much to ask. She knew this, and never came right out and told him, because she was scared of his reaction. One night when Hope was hunched over in pain, wondering whether she was in labour or not, she would call Victor's aunt, in fear, because Victor could not be reached. Was it a surprise that he was out drinking?

After a trip to the hospital, Hope found out she was experiencing Braxton Hicks, false contractions, but that the baby had dropped, which meant she was due any day now. Even this news wasn't enough to keep Victor at home, waiting, and sober. Hope would definitely try to use that to her advantage for a few days at least, but not without extra stress on her plate. Victor seemed unaware that stress on a pregnant woman can cause stress to the baby. Victor really needed a good smack upside the head, because this still wasn't all registering to him. He was so in over his head. The daddy title was still not defined in Victor's head.

Victor had always refused to fall into the cycle that he had seen in his family, but he also never realised the life he was leading, and was in complete denial to where he was heading with his choices and habits. Hope likewise refused to believe that Victor would fall into the pattern of his descendants, and she too was in denial, a tidbit naive, only seeing a slight glimpse of the bigger picture with each incident that took place because of his consumption. It would take years for Hope to really have clarity on the situation, and even then it was a bit of a blur what had happened and when. She did eventually see the true impact of alcohol and became repulsed by booze and its destructive capability. She herself, who once enjoyed a good night of drunken fun, could no longer be bothered to indulge in something which causes so many problems; breaking up families and stealing lives. Alcohol is such a powerful, and dangerous weapon, and that is just putting it mildly.

# CHAPTER FIFTEEN

HOPE HAD HEARD THE phrases, "Leave him . . . Get away . . . You can do better . . . and so on."

She had heard it all thousands of times, constantly, more and more as people saw Victor's dark side. All she had to do was reveal a small segment of their battles, and they were left in jaw-dropping disbelief. He was creating a charming reputation for himself, making a fool of himself and of her on a regular basis when he drank in public. Even his own friends had mentioned to Hope that he was becoming the guy nobody wanted around. Whether they were hinting at her to leave or just making a generalised observation, Hope knew that Victor was driving not only her, but everyone who mattered, away. This excruciatingly saddened Hope because Victor had been such a respectful child, whose mother was praised for raising such polite children. He had a well-established reputation in his hometown as a young man, and this was shameful.

People would tell Hope that she was "strong", that she was a wonderful mom and could do great things if she left him behind and got the negativity of alcohol out of the way. People knew that Victor's not-so-charming nature would only get in the way and would not be a healthy environment for Hope to raise Gracie. It should have been clear to Hope, and she should have left. The truth is though, sometimes people can see the facts, and people know the answers, but life is not as clear cut as math or science, and people have feelings. The brain's opinion and the hearts opinion are not always on the same page, and sometimes the clash between the two is so much to bear that it leaves even the most sensible, smartest person, unsure of which path to take. Hope was blindsided. She didn't want to believe what she was seeing.

Hope was a strong person in some means, but in this situation, all she knew was love. Her strengths came in strange shapes and sizes. The sappy romantic dreamer in her weakened her logic and common sense. Hope's poor heart was fragile, she always was a very emotional person, and she could be crushed at the slightest of a hit. Vulnerable, at risk, and defenceless. Hope would look around and see all the broken marriages, the people splitting up everywhere, and she was in awe at how easily they moved forward with life. People would change partners as often as their underwear, and well . . . that just wasn't Hope.

Hope had been hurt before, and each time she remembered feeling like each day was a challenge; getting out of bed each morning, getting dressed, eating, and especially breathing — it all felt like a chore. It took forever for her to feel like she was alive again, and not just existing. It literally felt like life was coming to an end. Falling, losing, failing . . . dying! When she met Victor, and their connection unravelled, she remembered having a sense of assurance, a sense of overwhelming faith that she would never have to feel that heart-wrenching brokenness ever again. Victor was her saviour, her hero, her soul mate, her everything. She had a strange sense of sureness, sureness that they had exactly what it took to last forever. Life and Victor would try proving her wrong. She just couldn't bear the thought of truly letting go, and going through that again. She would rather live miserably with Victor, and a false sense of hope, than to be totally ALONE. To Hope, being single was like admitting that she had failed. Failure as a title wouldn't be so bad, except for the pain and realness that came along with it. The loss, the fall, the ending.

While all the negativity of their lives was occurring, before that night of war, someone from the past crept back into Hope's life. When this old flame, the man she had been enticed by once before, started emailing her, Hope didn't beat around the bush. She flat out told him in writing that they were friends, strictly a platonic relationship, and could not return to the line they had crossed before. However, she also revealed the ugly truth of where her life was at, as they reconnected quickly through writing. He wasted no time in telling her he still thought about her all the time, and couldn't stop thinking about her, and that he really was in love with her. Right now, those were words that she wanted to hear so desperately, and she was seeking someone to fill the empty void in her heart.

Almost anyone could say those three little powerful words and bring a smile to Hope's weakness. This man saw her unhappiness as his chance to woo her off her feet and steal her over. She was down, and feeble, and he saw right through this. His flirtations were tempting, and hearing someone say they would be there, in a heartbeat, if that was what she wanted, was a confusingly happy-sad jive for Hope. It took her last few ounces of courage not to give in to the sweetness.

Hope did find herself fantasying about a perfect little family, with a step-dad. Exactly what she never wanted was now standing right in front of her, calling out to her. Though the word "step" scared her, the idea of a loving man was appealing. He was still in a relationship with someone else though, and despite his vows to leave her, Hope had heard the statistics and the high failure rate for relationships that stemmed from an affair. There would be trust issues, and Hope didn't think that was a healthy path to take, considering her current situation. What if this was what he did, and how he rolled, and what if he did the same thing to her? She already knew she was overly optimistic with people, so she was trying to use her common sense. She didn't need to go from one tainted love to another.

Hope also did not want to be the reason another woman felt the exact same pain she was feeling. The thought of how this man looked at her constantly though, when they worked together, was a thought she never got past, as she clearly remembered that seductive love in his eyes. The comfort he was bringing right now just with words on a screen was all so intense, and Hope wondered if someday this would be the man she could spend her life with. Husband material. The bigger problem was this man's name though . . . . it wasn't Victor.

Even if Hope allowed this fantasy to become real, she would spend the rest of her life trying to convince herself that she did the right thing. Even if she married him, the true family ties between him and her own family would not be what existed with Victor, and her in-laws might not be the same as what she would have in Victor's family. She had a once-in-a-lifetime bond with Victor's family, just as she thought she had with Victor. It might all work, but it would be a settle-for-less type of deal. The guilt of being a home-wrecker would never leave her either. She believed that she would always yearn for Victor, and that true happiness would never reside within her. She had learned that Victor was irreplaceable. She just wished that Victor felt the same way towards her.

For now, she would keep this man at a safe distance, but close enough, in case Victor made the decision for her, and in case he did push her away, without a choice. A friend to talk to, someone to confide in, and leverage against Victor. Hope knew the wrongness in that, but the whole situation left her doing things the old Hope would never do, things that were outright wrong. She was playing with fire. If she absolutely could not have Victor, and he chose to throw away their love, she had another road to take, potentially. Hope feared being alone, and this seemed like a safety net . . . her back-up plan. Love should never have a back-up plan, but Hope found power in her dirty mind games. Her games didn't work to her advantage with a drunk boyfriend. Victor was so deeply inebriated so often now that he didn't clue in to the jealousy Hope was trying to create, at least not in the way she wanted.

She was so deeply terrified of the hurt that would come from leaving him. What scared her even more was the thought that he wouldn't care, that after all the love they shared, he seemed like he would just move on, like the rest of the heartless idiots roaming the earth. She would fall apart, while he forgot her. If he fell in love again, it would kill her. She just wasn't that strong. She wanted Victor to mourn the way she did, over the loss of them. She was literally afraid to die of a broken heart.

Even though there was barely any relationship left between them, Hope wanted to cling to the tiny piece of THEM she still had. Part of her was pretending, trying to put up a front, living a lie. She would try to imagine her life without Victor, but she kept coming back to an image of him, the day they started their relationship journey, and she just kept trying to find her way back to those sunshiny days. With every ounce of fight she had left in her, she had to keep going. Maybe just a little longer. That was exactly how she had survived this long, and why she was still in this mess, constantly promising herself that she would wait just a little longer.

If Victor had cancer or some other critical illness, she wouldn't leave him, she would be there to look after him, by his side through it all, and she would try to help him pull through it. If she were chronically ill, she would hope that he would be there by her side, like he used to be through the hard times. Sometimes she would tell herself, "this isn't him, it is his disease arguing with me, and his disease can kiss my ass, because I am not leaving my Victor, the man hiding behind the mask." She would make herself feel better with these notions. This was one of her survival tactics. She knew if she tried to explain herself to anyone, that she would sound like a crazy lady. Some days she felt crazy, so she just tried to be her own therapist.

She was infinitely devoted, more than anyone could know. She knew that her love for Victor couldn't just be dissolved or washed away, and even if their destiny was separate, she would love him till the day she died. If she ever left, she knew time would make it more bearable, and Gracie would bring her joy every day, but she would never fully heal. She would be scarred forever, gruesome, unsightly scars. A piece of her heart would be missing, and trapped with Victor, whether he would realise that or not. Something would always feel incomplete. She desperately wanted her little girl to grow up with her father around, and not just stupid visitation, and Hope would get so infuriated at the thought of how any decisions she made now would have such a powerful effect on her daughter's future too. That was what she wanted Victor to comprehend.

# CHAPTER SIXTEEN

WHEN HOPE DISCOVERED SHE was pregnant, she was unsure how to react at first. It took a few minutes to really click in, and excitement came quickly thereafter, along with some fear and anxiety. Victor's initial reaction wasn't what Hope expected. He was away trucking and told her that he would have to call her back. He just needed to let the news sink in, and get into a safe zone before they could talk. He was cruising along on a busy highway, in his defence. However, Hope just felt the panic in his voice and didn't feel a sense of understanding support, as she assumed he would provide. He left her more worried than when she first realised the news.

Victor later gave Hope the support she had been seeking, and even became excited. Victor certainly admitted to his own fears and worries, but perhaps he didn't have the nerve to admit he really was not ready to be a father. Hope fell so in love with her unborn child and the idea of motherhood, and her excitement grew enormously. She was told by many people that she looked like the happiest pregnant lady there ever could be. She even loved her belly, and wore it proudly, however she was a little turned off by the stretch marks that now protruded from her stomach. She carried a glow from ear to ear, and couldn't wait for the reality to come to life. She was not at all prepared for the bout of postpartum depression that would strike her the day she came home from the hospital with Gracie.

Hope wasn't prepared for the inconsiderate nature of Victor, who would leave her feeling neglected. All she wanted was his companionship during this final, uncomfortable, less enjoyable stage of pregnancy and the newness of motherhood after birth. She wanted her partner, who conceived this child with her, to bask in their upcoming excitement. She wanted support, love, and a friend. Victor was cowardly out drinking away his fears and worries. Trying to get any attention, and a little affection was like pulling teeth for Hope. Victor was so insensitive and so withdrawn. Postpartum depression might have skipped her, had she not felt so alone.

Hope had never suffered from any type of depression in her lifetime, so this was completely out of context for her, and she did not understand the negative emotions that were looming overhead. "I wanted this so badly", she thought, as she laid in bed that night, wishing she could still be in the hospital just to have the support, the comfort, and the knowledge of the nurses. She felt like they pushed her out of there so quickly, and she was so tired, but too scared to ask for help. She wanted to be a good mom, but suddenly everything was all too real.

The word "Mom" had always been safe to Hope, her own mother being her rock for her entire life. She had big shoes to fill, and did not feel she could live up to her own standards. A tiny, fragile life was in her arms, literally, and her responsibility, and she suddenly felt so unprepared, and unready. No book put these feelings into words, nobody told her it would be so tough. Where did the excitement go? Faded away. She felt lost and overwhelmed, and mostly just really scared.

The walls were caving in around her, and she felt trapped, especially because the house they had recently moved into still had no sense of home to Hope. She remembered feeling like she needed to move back to her own parents house just to feel comfort and security and to be supported. She remembered watching other young moms, around her age, who appeared so happy, and she wished she could find that. She was expecting those feelings when she was awaiting Gracie's arrival, and now she had a beautiful, healthy little girl, whom some people would give anything to have, and thus, she was so ashamed of these feelings floating around inside her. There was such confliction taking place within her. She loved her new daughter greatly, and she didn't blame Gracie by any means, but she didn't think love should feel so sad. She could not share with anyone. Guilt ate away at her, and made her feel worse about everything. She didn't even want to talk to Victor, and she felt like he wouldn't understand if she tried.

That night, as Gracie slept for the first time in her new home, Hope would bawl her eyes out, as she absorbed the vastness of who she was now, and what she had to do. Change, so much change all at once, bombarding her. She was also terrified of Gracie, and although love consumed her, it was just such an overpowering love that is was frightening and intimidating. The fragility of a newborn baby is scary to a new young mom. She was scared to break her, to hurt her, to hold her wrong, to feed her wrong, to choke her, she was scared of SIDS (Sudden Infant Death Syndrome), scared that Gracie would stop breathing in her sleep, and she just wished that her little bundle would grow up a bit faster, and be a little easier to care for.

A very small part of Hope just wanted her carefree life back, and she couldn't admit that to anyone. The guilt of that thought shamed her, and made her feel so awful that she was grief-stricken. She already felt like she was a bad mother, this was just sickening. Victor suspected something wasn't right, and as he wiped her cheek he was answered by the wetness of her tears, asking with true concern, "Hope, what's wrong?"

"I don't know", was all Hope could squeeze out of her poor confused self. Victor's love reflected with his words, as he was still trying to be supportive at this stage in the game. He was worried, but really did not understand. Victor had to go back to work, and maybe Hope just wished for a few more days of his help, but he could not afford to take that time. Hope would become very lonely, and start to feel isolated by life. She felt the days drag on at first, for lack of sleep, constant feedings, changing, and tears. She cried her days away, as she held and rocked her little girl.

Hope felt very protective, but so scared to let her baby girl down, to hear her cry, and not to know what she needed. She would get very anxious when Gracie cried, like she couldn't soothe her quickly enough. When Gracie screamed, it startled Hope, every time, and gave her a panicky, heart—racing feeling.

Moms are not supposed to have these thoughts, moms are supposed to have it all together, and have all the answers. Hope had heard about the 'Baby Blues' and yet she was in denial, or just didn't understand. She was very good at hiding her torment, and every visitor who entered to meet her new addition was greeted with a smile and friendliness. Realistically, she wanted to be left alone.

Within weeks, most of these negativities would subside, and her blues would get brighter, and turn to more of a sparkly shade. She would accept the idea that motherhood is a mixture of fears and joys, but the fears cannot control us, or we will not appreciate or even realise the joys. Hope saw the joy now, and her love for Gracie grew stronger by the minute. She became completely engulfed in the title of motherhood and embraced in its delights. She wanted to spend every second holding her, and they spent the majority of their days sleeping together, building a beautiful close-knit bond in the recliner chair. People noticed and teased Hope for the constant kissing syndrome she had, kissing her daughter a million times a day. If Hope wore lipstick, her lip prints would be tattooed on her daughters entire body, head to toe. There was still something wrong though, as Hope let the house go to shambles, her own hygiene was questionable, and the TV and catnaps filled the hours of each day.

Hope felt so drained, and just wanted rest, constantly. She started to feel like Victor wasn't helpful enough. He complained at her lack of duties around the house. She wanted to be a good housewife, but had no energy. Victor was lucky to come home to a full course home-cooked meal, which was the extent of Hope's housewife duties for the day. When she started to realise how little she was doing, and the damage of this horrible routine she started, she became more ashamed, and the fights between her and Victor would start. He definitely didn't understand what was going on with her, and she knew she couldn't explain herself. Little arguments of blame and frustration infiltrated, and with the addition of Victor's dirty little habit, a war zone spiralled.

Hope wanted so badly just to be back in the comfort of her own childhood home, with the help of her mom. She would analyze other new moms and wonder or watch how much support they received, feeling a lack of partnership, teamwork, and support by far. She still felt foreign in the community to a certain degree, a sense of isolation. The guilt ate at her, and she would go walking often, just to escape the house, and the loneliness. She did feel lucky to have her sister, who had experienced similar feelings in her early days of motherhood, and felt they grew much closer through the time. They spent many hours bonding over the phone, often resulting in Hope blubbering like a baby, allowing her some relief.

Hope should have set aside her pride, and reached out to others, seeking help during her Baby Blues, because she would have learned that Postpartum is a typical and normal occurrence after having a baby. Motherhood and its newness is a lot to digest. Other moms may have been able to talk her through the hard times, and give her positive reinforcement for the better times to come. Hope definitely did place some blame on Victor, looking back. Her expectations during pregnancy had been different than what actually occurred following the birth of Gracie. Hope was exhausted, sore, and a hormonal mess of tears and joy. All typical experiences, but then when you add the stresses of alcohol, and the pre-existing issues between the two, and the lack of support she received from Victor, of course she had troubles.

Hope did not know how to reach out in a way that would get Victor to listen, to help, and just to be there. She had more faith in him to be there, prior to Gracie's birth, and he was really letting her down now. Hope wished Victor had been more compassionate during the trying times, and just there, literally by her side for company, so she wouldn't feel so stuck and tied down in this new life while he was out being free still, like nothing was new. He had always been the super supportive boyfriend, there when times were tough, but apparently this was just too much for him. As she fell more in love with her daughter, she drifted further away from Victor, because she didn't feel he was sharing the journey. She adjusted to the role of motherhood, remembering how pressured her life felt just a year ago.

Hope had been an over-achiever in high-school, the honour roll student who was supposed to make it big in life, and really be "somebody". She had major standards to live up to, and couldn't bear the thought of failure. That would have ruined her. Society sets the bar high when defining success, and Hope set her own standards equally high. Hope felt in over her head with stress at University. She worried about what others would think, now that she was dropping out of school due to pregnancy, but within months, she would enjoy the idea of the changes and adapt an attitude that "this is meant to be".

Hope also pushed the worries of what others thought aside now, because she herself was happy. It was hard to believe that the goody-two-shoed, teacher's pet, who wanted to please everyone else, would be the girl in the class to wind up pregnant, but she knew it was her destiny. She was a born mother. She became so proud of the mother she was, and she knew that it reflected. Hope was thankful for her "excuse" to leave school, though her pregnancy was unplanned, she now felt that her little girl was her "saving Grace", and that was how she chose her name.

"Unplanned, but wanted" would be her motto, as she never wanted her child to feel like a burden, or unloved. After six months of raising her little girl, now Hope would not change a thing. No regrets. An unexplainable, over-the-top love. Her little girl was golden, the best thing to ever happen to her. If she could change anything in her life, it would be Victor, and his drinking, and his damaging ways. He was so cowardly, hiding behind his bottle.

As the pleaser-type that Hope was, there was a brief phase during her postpartum days where she felt like she was being judged for every little thing she did, by her parents, and sometimes even by Victor's mom. She felt pressure to live up to their standards. Her parents, especially her father, left her feeling like a disappointment. She wanted to make everyone proud, but she felt her own father nit-picked at little things she did she as a new mom. She truly valued all of their opinions, but she didn't want to be controlled or lectured on parenting. She had to learn for herself. Advice is wonderful, but she needed to discover her own capabilities, which she did in due time. She looked back later, knowing that they wanted the best, and their intentions were not to degrade her, and their words of wisdom were just that, and they only cared for her best interest and that of Gracie's as well, but in her emotional state, it was overwhelming.

Hope was left questioning her own mothering skills, but only for a short time. She had high expectations for herself as a mom, as she always had for herself, with anything she did, but she soon gained such huge confidence in her mommy-hood. Nobody could tell her she wasn't good enough anymore, and she knew her parents were indeed proud, and that almost anyone should be proud of her, and she also knew now they never felt disappointed in her, and they were just guiding her through the difficult days. There is no handbook on parenting, and everyone makes mistakes, but Hope felt that she had succeeded, and her postpartum depression days were only a brief phase that she grew past, and that she could look back at knowing she had overcome.

# CHAPTER SEVENTEEN

OTHERHOOD CAME NATURALLY WITH time, if only being a spouse did too. Hope would watch other couples, other families, other people in general, and wonder what their lives were like. She especially targeted young families, with a new infant, people who modelled them. She wondered if they were happy. Did they fight? Did he drink? Did she always feel stressed and angry? Did any true love stories still exist? Hope had a bad taste in her mouth for love, thinking everyone must live similarly. There cannot be peace when two people live together, and are forced to join their lives into one. Why bother? When she did see a couple who appeared happy and in love with a new baby, she felt envious. Were they sincere, or just putting up a front for the public eye? She was jealous of the men who were waiting hand and foot on the mothers of their children, if that did exist.

Victor had lived his whole life in this town where they now resided, but Hope was building her life around his. He never saw that, and she felt he didn't appreciate or understand the sacrifices she made, that were easier for him. Sometimes Hope unconsciously resented Victor and his family for being so close, not that she wasn't close to her own family, connectively, emotionally, and intimately, but because she wished that her parents lived closer in her time of need. It was the physical distance that ate at her, and sometimes felt like a million miles away. She yearned to have her mother at her side a little more, as she struggled with the postpartum days. Something about becoming a mother can actually make you into a big baby again.

She just wanted the extra support and comfort, but from her own family, not his family. However, this was not their faults, and they were loving and supportive people, and eventually she would feel guilt towards these feelings, and gratitude for having them, but she needed to adjust to all the newness. Time. She did adjust, very well, she felt. She fit in quickly enough, and made friends.

When Hope was pregnant, and they were trying to take charge of the situation, Hope and Victor had the chance to buy a house together, but the catch was, it was Victor's home-town. Hope was agreeable with this idea, and didn't give it another thought. They basically just danced through everything, floating, going through the motions to do what needed to be done. Now she had built up her own little niche, a life of her own around his, making mommy friends at the park, establishing a daycare out of their home, and networking to have adult contact, by befriending other childcare providers and young moms.

Hope grew closer again to Victor's family, as she got past her postpartum insanity, and appreciated their help and support. She rekindled the friendship in Victor's mom, though it was never really lost. Of course, all this just made it harder, when times got really tough between her and Victor, because she couldn't just run back to her parents or away from everything that defined her life. She had a life here now, and obligations to fulfill, and she was proud of the fact that she took charge to all this. Maybe that was a blessing in disguise.

Was Hope buying time, or driving a bigger wedge? She had such a need to maintain all her roles, and hold it together. She camouflaged her pain, but the living hell she hid so well caught up to her at night, almost every day. She feared the night, she feared the dark, and she feared being alone with herself and her house, and her big old empty bed. She needed the busyness, and that was probably her saviour during daylight hours. She could pretend to the world that her life was oh-so-great. She had milestones and facets that kept a sense of normality, and made life bearable.

Hope had no trouble starting her own family childcare home, starting small, but growing big rapidly. Family friends of Victor's mom had needed childcare, and this was right up Hope's alley, as she had been considering starting her own daycare anyway. This paved the way for her to do exactly that, and she enjoyed the hustle and bustle, giving her a sense of routine, a sense of purpose which she was proud of, and playmates for Gracie. She did not want to leave her baby girl and find a job outside her home, as she decided early on in motherhood. The idea of running a daycare just made sense to Hope. Mothering had become a breeze, as Gracie was truly a great kid, a great sleeper, super happy, and a highlight to her mom's life, and she felt like she was enriching both their lives by bringing extra kids into the home. She thought of it as hers and Gracie's daycare, their project together, a team effort.

The two boys that Hope started out with were also well-behaved, great little boys. Danny and Mark were Gracie's buddies, and planted their seeds in Gracie's heart, as they were very affectionate with her, and treated her like a little sister. They bonded, and Hope knew they could potentially be lifelong friends to Gracie. Hope knew from the time she first started watching the daycare providers at the park, when she took baby Gracie down for walks with a friend, she had found a calling for herself.

Hope had always dreamed of being an elementary teacher from a very young age, and that plan was bombarded with pregnancy, but perhaps someday Hope would still make it happen. In the meantime, looking after children, teaching them, guiding them, and filling her days at home with Gracie sounded like a great idea. It may help her in the long run. Hope explored and inquired with the ladies at the park, made the necessary calls, attended orientations, had visits with a coordinator who oversaw her facility to ensure that regulations were followed, that the kids were safe and healthy, and that her home was up to standards. Hope made the necessary changes, with Victor's help on the house, and never even needed to advertise.

By word of mouth, her name got out, and within a few months, she developed a positive reputation as a caregiver. She received calls off the hook, from people needing care for their children, and before she even knew what she'd gotten into or had a chance to take it all in, she was a licensed family care provider, with a house full of kids. She had playmates for Gracie, her own income, and a fulfilling sense of balance and routine. She was working at a college course, a requirement in the licensing process, which also made her feel good about herself. Her little business, along with chatting with moms at the park, gave Hope a sense of belonging, in the community. The park was her favourite place, as she loved watching children play and interact, all the while allowing mothers some adult contact and fresh air, to escape the house for awhile. A little vitamin D can do wonders.

Another factor that kept Hope from running away was their dog, another connection that they shared, something they had embraced together, but another thing that became Hope's responsibility when Victor became useless around their home, and sometimes another stressor in Hope's eyes. Hope and Victor had often had a chat about whether or not to get a dog, and the answer always leaned towards 'yes'. They had both grown up with dogs in their families, their childhood four-legged friends. They wanted Gracie to have the unconditional love of a fury friend too, as she grew up with a puppy, almost like a sibling.

One afternoon, Victor brought a tiny puppy home from his grandpa's farm, and Hope really should not have been surprised, but it was an adjustment. The trials and tribulations of a puppy, as Hope soon discovered, were more difficult than a newborn baby, as far as Hope was concerned. Whimpery nights and messy carpets left Hope wondering what they had gotten themselves into, but she did fall in love with this idiot mutt, and stuck it out, despite her rants. They would make constant jokes about their inbred farm mutt, whose father was her brother, justifying her idiosyncrasies, all the while watching Gracie fall in love too, and make a companion in Heidi.

Heidi, the dog, also bonded with Gracie, jumping into her lap, making her giggle and grin. She also claimed Gracie's belongings as her own too, jumping into the swing, her seat, and snuggling with her clothing, toys, and blankies, and of course chewing up several of Gracie's belongings too. Heidi was protective, but she certainly played a little too rough. Likewise, Gracie gave Heidi a run for her money, but they both quickly learned the word "Gentle" as they became best of buddies.

A dog, an infant, and now an overgrown childish drunken spouse; to say the least, Hope had her hands full. Sometimes this kept her busy enough that she didn't have time to over-analyse or even comprehend how bad it really was. She knew she would enjoy all this more if Victor and her could get things straight though, because their distance kept her living in limbo. Her future was considerably questionable, and she was just waiting for a little more structure and answers, one way, or another. If things with Victor were different, if they were better, like old times, then she would really have life made, but there always has to be a catch. He needed to grow up and find himself. Hope had to maintain control, despite everything and anything, because that was the type of person she was now, ever since she became a mom. She had the nature to nurture and care, and her feelings just had to stand back.

# CHAPTER EIGHTEEN

T O SOME, HOPE MAY have come across as an over-bearing stick in the mud. She might have sucked all the fun out of partying if Victor's friends or drinking buddies ever heard her argue her case. Hope used to know how to tie one on too though, and she had some crazy times that were talked about for years to come. Hope didn't take cheap taxies when she went out on the town for a good time. She thought ambulances were more exciting, and flirting with the paramedic while your boyfriend is at your side is even more entertaining. Maybe a night in a hotel would be fun . . . or even better, a night in the hospital is cheaper. Imagine being told you have to eat a soda cracker before you can leave, and be stuck in that dingy room all day, waiting for the Dr. to say you can be free again and that you had suffered from a minor case of alcohol poisoning. Her stomach need not be pumped because she was able to vomit enough to rid herself of the toxins.

Hope had her share of stories to tell, and some were humorous, but all in all, as a mom, she had no time or irresponsibility left in her for those adventures anymore. She was actually embarrassed by some of those stories, but they were nothing compared to the stories Victor created almost every weekend.

Like several teens, Hope drank just to get drunk, once upon a time, to let loose, to fit in, and for the fun — the stupid, reckless, drunken fun — but she was so beyond that now. She didn't have the desire anymore, partially because of Gracie, and the need to be responsible twenty-four hours a day, seven days a week. If something ever happened to Gracie, during just one night of being drunk, Hope would not forgive herself. She always had to feel in control of herself. The other reason was obvious, Victor, and all the chaos, and the negative repercussions, and she did not need to be the female version of that kind of wonderful. The fun was forgotten, and Hope was wrecked and distraught. She had actually grown to hate alcohol.

Betrayal is such a dirty word, such a dirty feeling, and such a dirty thing to cast upon someone. Of all the emotions Hope felt, betrayal summed up everything. A hit below the belt, unforgivable deeds, the climax of their story. Totally victimized. Victor had the upper hand, the control, the ability to leave Hope feeling meaningless, small, and as if she was the bad guy. Somehow she was left blaming herself, just like he blamed her. Pining for the answers, her entire outlook on life was turned completely upside down.

Hope and Victor were existing in complete dysfunction and tyranny. Their lives lacked balance, discipline, management, efficiency, and a partnership that should exist in parents. Hope was presented with multiple challenges, which she had to recognize. She needed to identify that she was lessening her chances at ever being successful if she allowed negative aspects to rule their lives. If Victor was going to continue allowing alcohol to influence his life, along with other unfulfilling behaviours, Hope had to step back. She could no longer let herself get dragged down with him. She had responsibilities. She was the backbone in the household already, but she needed to rise above, and try maintaining a stiff upper lip, making sure Gracie's best interest was the biggest aspect to consider. She could no longer be humiliated by him, or neglected.

Change can be a horrible, sad thing sometimes. Hope had been such a positive and happy person for as long as she could remember, until recently, and now she was grey and dull; the experiences of her life had left her optimism confused, and fading. So tired of pretending. Tired of dreaming. Tired of fighting. Tired of waiting for things to get better. Just played out and down-right exhausted. Feeling so drained just didn't feel worth her while anymore. Giving up was almost starting to sound easy now. This had gone too far. Hope had endured more than she thought any person should have to, in the way of hurt and hardships. Yet facing the world alone still sounded scary. The title of single mom really took it's toll on her thoughts, leaving her torn on what to do and where to turn.

Hope wished she could just return to the simplicities and innocence of her own carefree childhood. The days when the real issues were placed on her parents, and they would fix everything and anything. She knew that her mom and dad had no place in fixing this mess, and in fact, they were so far out of the loop of her struggles and emotion now. She couldn't begin to explain to them, and she was actually saving them from the worry and stress. Funny how things change when you enter adulthood, perhaps more so when you give birth to your own offspring, and suddenly realise that parents are just people too, trying to get by and make the best for their children. She adored her parents with these thoughts, and just wished they really did have the power to make the pain go away, just like they could do so magically when she was little. Her parents had done well with her, so how did she let herself fall into this ugliness? She was so ashamed again.

Hope just wanted to be special again, to Victor. She didn't want to be just another girl in his lifetime. She was the mother of his child, but she wanted to be that and more. She wanted to feel remarkable, and to know that she had left her prints etched into him forever. She visualized her handprints, footprints, fingerprints, and even lip prints plastered and smeared all over his heart. She didn't want another woman to ever have the chance to get close to him, that would crush her more than anything else. She wanted to leave her branding so others would back off. Happiness, she knew, could come in many shapes and sizes. She never would have imagined as a child, or even a year or two prior, that her life would be so painstaking. She wanted to attain some uncompromised happiness again. Some days it felt like just yesterday, some days it felt like a lifetime ago. There was no way in hell that Hope could ever stop loving Victor, but that was all she really knew for certain. The rest was ambiguous and blurred.

# CHAPTER NINETEEN

EMEMBER THAT HOSPITAL STAY that Hope had a few years back? All the testing she underwent still left unanswered questions. Sometimes Hope still suffered silently from strange symptoms, discomforts and abnormalities. Her body was playing games with her, and she tried to ignore it, as she felt that was best for now. She would feel like her legs 'fell asleep' far too easily, and felt tingly or numb. Sometimes it was her hands, and she knew her circulation had always been terrible. She was always cold, especially her hands and feet. Her hands would turn funny colors, pretty shades of purple and blue, and her reflexes were weak as doctors had pointed out, and Hope could see for herself.

The doctors had mentioned the possibilities of MS, especially due to the questionable areas that had appeared on Hope's brain on her MRI results. Some doctors referred to the spots as "plaque", others called it "lesions". All Hope thought of when she first heard the phrases, in fear, was teeth and dental terms. Since when did plaque build-up on a brain? Her brain had dirty patches of gunky build-up in the mental depiction her imagination invented. Some doctors simplified the terms as white patches which may be early signs of MS or other health issues. They could be nothing, but they could also be something.

First, Hope was in denial, and secondly, she was scared, but started dealing in a tough manner. She researched, and carried on with life in the mean time. She went to testing, and appointments, neurologists, specialists, and was even sent to an MS clinic. She was told that they were fairly certain she may have MS, but as time went on, they ruled out the idea, because she was doing well and there were no changes with the spots on her brain. Later Hope would question why they never took into account that pregnancy can actually put MS into remission, and perhaps her lack of symptoms connected to her recent child. The one specialist who was supposed to be a great, well-known specialist had told Hope she was "99% certain that she had MS", and those words would always stay with Hope. You do not forget something like that. No definite answer could be given, but "99%", well on that day, that seemed definite enough.

Hope felt fine for so long though, and motherhood needed her completely, so she could not waste much time wondering about her health, when there didn't seem to be an issue anymore. Nothing extreme. She chose to live life normally, until more need for concern, if any. She still feared the future, and wondered if some neurological disorder would pop up at her. Victor's mother suffered from MS, ironically enough, but the positive side of that was that he knew what it was, and he had promised her he'd be at her side, no matter what. At the time, that was a huge strength, and exactly what she needed. Now, it seemed like a lie. She didn't want to ever need that type of help or support, but the present fear laid in the fact that she didn't feel Victor was capable of caring for himself, let alone anyone else.

What if? What if something was wrong, if anything happened to her . . . she feared for Gracie's sake, whether her daddy, Victor, could get himself together, and be the man he would need to be, in such a circumstance. She prayed that she would never have to find out the hard way, if he had that potential. Sadly, she was doubtful, and terrified for her daughter. She had to maintain good health and strength. She tried to be optimistic most of the time, but lately, optimism was like catching a falling star. The odds were not really on her side. Her whole world seeped with negativity. She could not control Victor, but she wanted to believe in him, and his potential to get help and be himself again, a great person.

Hope still wanted to live out her dream, to get married, and to live a family life-style. These days that dream seemed far-fetched. Could that ever happen, or was she doomed to be a single-mom, or the girlfriend who lived like a fool and waited for a full-commitment forever, while her not-husband carried on like a kid? She couldn't marry a man she couldn't trust, and she couldn't marry a man who couldn't understand what marriage meant or appreciate what it included. She did not want to be a fool, but she didn't want to give up on the man she loved, not yet, truthfully, not ever. The changes that would have to happen to ever get to her dream goals in life would have to be extreme and radical, and Victor had no interest in any of those things. He couldn't even accept where they were at in their lives. He couldn't even get through a day without a fight, nor could Hope. They were so bitter with each other, and on different pages of life. Who could help them, or was this a cold case, beyond any professionals ability to reconcile?

# CHAPTER TWENTY

J UST WHEN HOPE THOUGHT her reminiscing was running out of recaps, and that it was only ugliness reigning now, along came another loving memory. The highs and lows had been resonating through Hope all day, and one more moment of proof cast back to the genuine kindness Victor once was. Hope did everything whole-heartedly, whether it be hard hits of bad times bashing in on her delicate soul, taking an intense beating, or high times of good gushing out of her, with nothing but love to share.

When Hope's niece got ill, at the young age of two, experiencing high fevers, extreme diarrhoea and vomiting, and worst of all, seizures, it was a trying and terrifying time for the family. Hope was devastated at the worry that something serious may be wrong with that poor little girl. She whole-heartedly struggled to keep composure, as she broke down in fear. Her poor sister, who had already lost a baby could not stand to lose another child, and did not deserve this strain and pressure. Hope's heart broke for all of them, and for herself. She loved her niece, like her own child, and would do anything for that precious baby girl, Alyssa. She would take her place in a heartbeat.

Halloween night this innocent child was missing out on a traditional childhood event, stuck sick in the hospital. She was poked and prodded, undergoing tests, and the helplessness and hopelessness that Hope felt made her ill too. She wanted to cancel Halloween. If her little angel couldn't celebrate properly, then why should anyone else be allowed. She was panicked and flustered and irrational, but only because she wanted everything to be ok. Her pain made her slightly bitter, but she drove to visit Victor that night because she didn't want to be alone and cry all night in solitude.

Victor also loved Hope's niece, who was a niece to him too, as he had been there since her birth, as Uncle Vic. He too was worried, and felt awful for the family. He stood by Hope's side that evening, drying her tears, and trying to console her, as much as he could. He couldn't undo the unfairness, and Hope was in a horrible mood, hard to deal with, but he could hold Hope and tell her he loved her, and that he wanted everything to be ok. Just having his company made it a little easier to get through the night until she could hear more on the status of Alyssa, her poor niece. The supportiveness of Victor was as whole-hearted as Hope, making them a great match. He truly was Hope's best friend, who knew her inside and backwards, better than she knew herself sometimes.

Where do you turn when your best friend, the person you usually run to with the tough stuff . . . is the tough stuff. When your best friend turns on you, and is no longer on your side, what CAN you do? That is when the world feels like it is over. Hope would have felt like her world really was done, but thank-god for Gracie, her new best friend, the new soul mate she herself had proudly created and was now raising. She had a new unconditional love and companion, but that didn't mean her heart wasn't throbbing the loss. She missed that love, that kindness, that support, and that place to run. She missed her best friend. She couldn't exactly pour her heart out to her infant daughter.

Hope spent that afternoon cuddling, tickling, playing, and laughing with her daughter. The sincere joy that someone so little could bring her was a huge comfort. She knew that Gracie and her shared an unconditional love, and that was such a calming feeling, which she needed right then. Gracie's love brought tears to her mother's eyes, as they hugged, and Gracie's tiny little hand patted her mother on the back, as if to say, "We'll be ok momma".

Hope knew then, if Gracie was all she had left of this little family that they had created, she would survive, because her daughter would give her the strength. Did she really want to believe in this notion? Not at all, but her and Grace would live a good life, because that was Gracie's right, and Hope would make damn sure that she never disappointed her daughter as much as she felt she was now. She felt such a strong aching that she was letting her little girl down, and yet she knew that Gracie had no clue, thankfully. It was her job and duty and privilege to make sure that her daughter was cared for, but in the best environment she could give to her, to make her happy. Maybe that environment had to be away from her daddy, unfortunately.

Soon enough, Gracie would be older, and she would start to understand the world around her. Hope wanted Gracie to feel the beauty of life, to know that there was a positive side to this world, and not to grow up depressed and closed-minded to the possibilities of love. A twinge of strength soared through Hope at that moment. The grief within her retracted just a smidgen. Gracie's smile warmed Hope's soul, with a sense of tranquility, and calmness replacing the depression that had been setting in earlier that day. She couldn't let Victor's selfish stupidity, or her own for that matter, hinder her spirited little girl. That was a beauty that needed to be nurtured and preserved and allowed to fly high. Her daughter possessed such splendour and soul, that was evident at her early age, and Hope knew this was not just her biased motherly opinion. Hope was scared to watch that greatness be stolen away, and it was her duty to guard and protect Gracie from these evils.

# CHAPTER TWENTY-ONE

RACIE WAS ALREADY LEARNING to mimic. She clapped, she gave 'high fives', she blew kisses, and now she was tickling her mommy. Her spongy little mind was absorbing the world around her, each day a lesson learned. She also liked to hum when she got tired. Right on cue, Gracie started to fuss, and as Hope rocked her precious girl and rubbed her own face into Gracie's soft velvety cheeks, a pleasant and gentle little hum protruded. Music that warmed the cockles of Hope's body, a sensually soothing sound.

"Mmm....naaa....naaa....hmm", squeaked from the little mousy mouth. Hope quietly hummed along with her daughter, as emotion consumed her yet again, and a lump formed in her throat. As Gracie drifted into slumber, a morsel of happiness blended with a hint or two of hurt, and rained down from Hope's eyes, dampening her cheeks, like a little squirt bottle. The squirt bottle upgraded to a super soaker within seconds though, and she could probably fill the ocean, and maybe even overflow it, as tears just kept streaming. She cried, and cried, and cried . . . and cried some more.

It was getting late, the day had passed, somehow, and Hope had been pre-occupied by the voices of the past that were bellowing out around her. Evenings were the worst though, as Hope's smidgen of peace went down with the sun. The house was quiet, Gracie was quiet, and Hope was left all alone with her thoughts, and the sound of her own heart beating rapidly, pulsating into the world of gloom. The darkness washed over her, like a gloomy shadow of grey and black, and she was reminded of how alone she truly was. She could not wrap her head around the loss of control she had over her life, considering she was the type A person who always had control over herself up until the past year. Frazzled, but controlled, and now, a mumble-jumbled disaster. She hoped she was delusional and that her life was normal, none of this had really happened, right? She could just pick up her socks, dust off her knees, and keep on trucking, right? No, this bad day had stemmed from a bad week, from a bad month, into a bad year.

Hope didn't even know who to reach out to, who to call, where to begin, for she had been trying to hide the truth for so long, only revealing little portions of the secret troubles she was living through, harbouring the skeletons in the closet, putting up a front, probably all the while keeping herself convinced. Today, she had managed to do her daily household duties, which allowed her mind to rest at least briefly. She had to keep herself busy, and Gracie helped, but still, she couldn't run from reality forever. It always found her when she tried. In a daze, Hope took Gracie to bed, returning to the couch, because she was scared to face her bed alone, which would signify Victor's absence, like a big kick in the head. She wasn't ready to deal with everything all at once. Avoidance in spurts, and acceptance in small doses, was probably the key to getting through.

Mothers are supposed to be the foundation that hold a family together, but Hope was hanging on by a few measly threads, and Victor was a fixture that was in need of maintenance. Hope wasn't qualified anymore, nor did she know where to go for help, to repair a broken man. Hope never wanted perfection, she knew that wasn't life, but she never expected this either. Bad hair days, headaches, snow storms, flat tires, sick kids, and spilt milk; those were supposed to be the minor imperfections of life. The ruts that leave people whining at the end of the day. The things we shrug off, and a good night sleep can ease, sometimes just a relaxing bath from a stressful week can make us feel as good as new. Feeling so rundown by someone who once cared though, that was worse than anything. This couldn't be fixed with a rest, a hot bath, a good wash, some Tylenol, a new tire, a doctor, or a little soap and water and a scrub. This was a little more serious. This was as real, rough, and as raw as it gets.

Hope was awoken early into the night, by the front door closing, as Victor uneasily walked in. Guilt was written all over his face, and shame was painted right down to his feet. Neither spoke, and he didn't even look at her for more than a split second. The way he held himself, the slumpish tone of his body language spelled out sorrow and hurt. Hope's body trembled and anxiety swarmed over her. She froze, unsure what to say, or what to do, and unable to move, sinking further down into the couch. She wished she could disappear. She wondered what all the rummaging and rustling noises were coming from the bedroom, where Victor had quickly jetted off to. "We can't keep living like this", Victor spoke, breaking the nervous silence, as he made his way back into the living room.

"I know", Hope agreed, reluctantly. Numbness swarmed back through her, when she noticed the bag in Victor's hand. Reality sunk in, as Victor made his way to the door, and Hope was fighting with all her might not to cry. Her airway felt constricted, like her body was suffering from anaphylaxis. She was allergic to pain. She had lost him, and suddenly she wanted to run to him, jump at him, and hold him tight and close. All the anger vanished, and all she felt was love for him again. Her heart was skipping a beat again, just like in the early days, and her pulse was intensifying rapidly. This was all too dramatically real, a bitter sweetness.

It was too late, she felt defeated. Her heart was crumbling like a cookie in the hands of a small child. Little did she know, Victor was also breaking, and on the brink of death. If there was a cliff, he may have leapt, without a second thought. He was trying to be strong, and his brain was telling him that it was best for now to walk out the door and not look back. His heart, however, was on the same page as Hope's, beating itself up for allowing this upheaval to get so out of hand. The chemistry they once shared gushed out from somewhere deep within, and he too wanted to grasp Hope into his arms. He was ashamed of last night's uproar, ashamed of the waters they had been rowing for far too long. He was ashamed of who he had become. This was not the behaviour of a man, he knew. This wasn't even the behaviour of a boy. This was beyond wrong, and he was so guilt-stricken and sick with regret.

Victor no longer felt welcome in their home, and he felt he was out of place to try making amends at this point. He asked to see Gracie, not sure Hope would let him, and not sure he deserved to, but Hope just nodded. She knew if she spoke, she would break down, and she didn't have the energy to cry again. Weakness succumbed her. She just wanted to get past the breaking point of Victor leaving, because the wait was killing her inside.

It pained Hope that Gracie didn't have a say, and that Gracie would never have the chance to feel the love of a family unit, and that love would always be polluted from here on in. It pained her that Victor was giving up on himself. He was letting alcohol stand in the way of opportunities and chances. Hope had grown up with parents who were together, and to her that was right. Of course, there was moments of stress, and differences in opinion, but you work things out, you figure it out, you carry on, you learn and grow as a couple, and you live true to your vows, or to your children, whichever comes first, or both. That was the ideal lifestyle to Hope. She could not come to terms with the idea of how people just move forward, making it look so easy, forgetting their loved ones in the dust. Perhaps she just had a particularly fragile heart in comparison to the rest of the world, but to her it seemed so inexcusably wrong and unjust.

It seemed unfair to Hope, that failure is so typical in this day and age, and that parents force suffering upon their children at such a young age. Some are born right into it, just a slam dunk, with no alternative. To hope, that seemed ridiculous and low, all out of selfishness, immaturity, and irresponsibility, and Hope just wished for better. A stinging wish. "Why can't we all just grow the F**K up, instead of robbing our children of their carefree childhood, and stealing their innocence. We bring them into this world, and we are supposed to give them unconditional love and protect them, and one of their first lessons is pain, and the fallacy of love," thought Hope.

Hope sat there, blankly staring into the wall, with a solemn look of disgust.

Embittered thoughts trailed through Hope's mind, such as, "We show them broken promises, broken dreams, and we expect them to do better . . . well that is asking a lot . . . that is setting the bar high, isn't it? We should just push them out of the birth canal, and set them down on the floor to walk, better yet lets send our newborns out on their own, to learn to fend for themselves, that would be logical, and possible, right?" To Hope this deadbeat nature seemed just as insane as these ideas sounded. "Society is a failure", thought Hope, yearning to live in an era where simplicity was the only way; the day and age where a candle lit the way to a new day.

# CHAPTER TWENTY-TWO

HOPE REMEMBERED BELIEVING IN magic and thinking the world was perfect in her youth, and feeling like her parents could fix anything that was ever wrong or broken. Her life was always full of treasures and blessings, and she never knew any huge degree of disappointment. She just wanted Gracie to believe in magic and perfection for awhile, and she was so utterly disappointed that she was robbing her of these virtues before she could even feel the carefree ideology.

"Adults are just overgrown children, only without the ability to truly enjoy the simplicities of life, and with more stupidity on our shoulders," thought Hope, in an outrage. Her dissatisfaction towards the entire world at large was suddenly paused, at the sight of Victor caressing their daughter's little blonde ringlets. This view emphasised the waste of the circumstances, and although a little trace of happiness trickled over her, just as quickly, grief slammed back down on her, as she acknowledged the forthcoming loss. Hope wished there was a pause button, to freeze this moment, just for a little while. This was beautiful.

The lives of Victor and Hope were in derailment. Victor had been living in a trans of hypnosis, jiving through an out-of-body experience. Hope still had to cling to the idea that this was only a temporary deterrent, and like when being hypnotised, Victor would snap out of it soon. Victor should take this moment and lock onto it, and learn from it, and see that he was throwing this beauty away. He should notice that it was time to stop playing games. This should be that finger-snapping, back to reality moment. If he didn't play his cards right, this would be gone all too soon. This moment should be enough, but Hope could sense that it wasn't, not for Victor. Not quite. It was much more complex that just figuring out what he had. As far as Victor was concerned, he did realise the loss, but how could he unspeak the cruel words of months gone by, and how could he undo the damage and the pain. It felt way too late.

Hope adored the two people in her presence, more than anything in the world, but them as a family, unfortunately felt like it was an un-detainable goal. The greatness of being a mom was the best joy life could offer, and Hope wanted so desperately to share that greatness with Victor, and for him to feel the same way about being a dad. If only Victor had some insight, some prophecy to the sunshine his daughter would someday deem him to be, in her eyes he would still be her superhero, and that is all a little girl knows. Hope had once sought out Victor as her superhero too, and he lived up to those standards for awhile, but her hero was poisoned now, and his vision of life was clouded and hazy.

Picture perfect summed things up, but that was the problem. In a photograph, it was a beautiful sight, but behind the scenes, there was more than what met the eye, and it was not pretty. Hope knew that very shortly, Victor planned to walk out the door, and her dreams would go up in smoke, and she would be left in the rubble to pick up the pieces of her shattered heart. Truthfully though, she knew they were equally responsible for the downfall. She felt such tremendous sadness, for herself, and for Gracie, and even for Victor. One day, he would wake up and realise what he had lost, but she couldn't wait for that day. This was no life. She wanted him back NOW, and her patience was finished. She missed him now, she took pity on him now, but she could not play these games any longer.

Hope would give almost anything to get back to the undeniable chemistry, and the euphoric serenity that once danced amongst them. The ache of long lost times, and what could have been, loomed over Hope. She yearned to feel his warmth against her, the tenderness of his kiss, the smoothness of his skin, and the elation of his breath as their bodies linked in harmony.

Those times made life a treasure, but now Hope was dying inside, and all she wanted to do was shriek, and scream, and of course, cry. She could probably have a world record, person to cry most in a twenty-four hour period. Her tear ducts should be dried out by now, the low fuel light should be beeping and blinking at her. Cupid needed his neck rung, for allowing them to ever cross paths. Serendipity could kiss her ass, because this was cruel, and nobody should ever feel such torture. Hope felt imprisoned, persecuted, and as though she was waiting on death row; a very dragged out execution, a full-blown tragedy.

As she watched Victor lay their daughter back down into her crib, she contained her feelings, knowing there was no point in stirring up a fight now. This wasn't what Hope wanted, but the Victor she knew and loved had been gone for awhile. Gracie cried, as if to say, "Please daddy, stay." Victor decided to change her diaper and make her a bottle, just because he was trying to stop time, and make the most of what would probably be his last night at home, all while Hope stood by and watched like a zombie. A sombre little sigh crept out. "I know you won't believe me, but I am sorry, Victor blurted.

"Me too," Hope chocked out. They exchanged a pitiful glance, followed by a long, lost stare. It was like looking into a mirror; their eyes, they all contained the same agony, both his and hers. The awkward silence returned. Victor set Gracie into her swaying baby swing, with her bottle, turning on the musical setting, bending down to give her a long, drawn-out kiss. Gracie's music had never sounded so loud to her, as if the music was trying to drown out Hope's emotion. She wanted to dissolve into the music, and disappear into the clouds. The music was Hope's escape, the tiny safety net she needed. The music paused, shifting notes, and throwing Hope back into reality. Victor scooted over to the door, and tried to put on his shoes in a hustle. His hands were shaking, and he was fighting the urge still, to hug Hope. This was one of the saddest hours of Victor's life, and he could not find the words to say what he truly wanted to say. His throat felt sticky, and dry all at the same time.

What Hope did not see was how hard Victor was fighting not to cry. At that very moment, he felt love again. They were connected by their disconnection. They both felt such a flustered panicky feeling, like they were at gunpoint, with no where to run. As Hope sauntered back to the couch, sitting down beside Gracie, Victor forced himself to exit, fast. The sound of the door closing was the last blow that pushed Hope's rickety heart over the edge, back into tears. She sobbed—deep, pathetic sobs. A few minutes later, Victor walked back through the door, and one sight of Hope, made his soul rupture and weep in sorrow too. He just couldn't bear to walk away from her, knowing her state. He found worse than expected when he walked back in. He wanted to surrender himself, and fix everything, but life just felt so complicated.

"I am so sorry, but I will just keep hurting you . . . I am just going to stay at my dad's for awhile . . . until we figure things out. I have to, I am sorry, really Hope," Victor managed to mumble out through his cries. Hope just nodded, not finding the words amidst her tears. She wanted to stop him, grab him, and hold him as tight as ever, and never let go. She wished they could undo the last few months, and rewind back to their better days, a few edits and deletions here and there, and they could create the perfect love story again. The love was still there, and they were affirming this with the waterworks plummeting like a fountain, from both their faces. Hysterically crashing and burning. Treacherously beautiful. It was a gut-wrenching, heart-throbbing, 'can't watch', 'can't imagine', type of moment.

# CHAPTER TWENTY-THREE

HE STAINED TICKS OF the clocks from their past were washed away, replaced by the arrow-shaped hands on a heart-shaped clock, ticking to the beat of a love song. The irony in this moment of pure sadness leading its way to great joy was unimaginable. They shed the most intimate tears in history, as their souls both melted-down in sync. Victor and Hope's unwritten future was less vague instantaneously in this defining moment.

Maybe, just maybe, they could fix this. Maybe it wasn't too late. Hope knew that as hard as it would be, they would have to be strong enough to stay apart for awhile, to process, and not rush back into a repetition of their adversity, and she knew it was for the best. At least her brain was telling her that; if she listened to her heart, she would have believed in the magic of that moment. She had to be careful not to be too optimistic though, because she knew she might get her hopes up, and set herself up for another setback. Could they mend their broken bridges? First they would have to be cruel, to be kind. A good strong dose of tough love. They had to see if absence truly could make their hearts grow fonder.

Have you ever seen a blue moon? The English language is a funny thing. A figure of speech . . . what does that even mean? Does a blue moon come out when pigs fly? Hope had been waiting for the little porkers to flap their wings for quite some time, and as she looked out the window at the starry sky, she could have sworn the moon was blue and shadows of winged little runts floated past. Just as fast as life can go from wonderful to ugly, it can go right back to grand! You just never know! Hints of magic had been caught in various moments of Hope's and Victor's life, and Hope saw them, but Victor never seemed to understand. She just viewed everything different. When she had been pregnant with Gracie, only one person could ever get that unborn baby girl to kick her momma's guts the way her daddy's touch triggered. She knew him from the start. There was a love connection like no other between father and daughter, just like there was between Hope and Victor. The magic was always there, always.

Hope had a say now, and a voice in the matter again. Hope was a juror in the courtroom of Victor's life. Only a small percentage of the verdict rested in her hands, and Victor's plead could actually decipher her call. The other jurors included Victor's alter—egos; he, himself, and him, and one higher being who would make the final call. Victor had made his bed, and it was too late to refuse judgement. Maybe with the right outcome, they could get their groove back. We just never know what life has in store, but the thing about life is that if it was too predictable all the time, that might take away from the point in living. Life is about not knowing, and the uncertainties, and with the right frame of mind that can be exciting. The subtle little hints can lead us to exhilarating highs of anticipation and joy. Sometimes we don't have a say in the outcome of life, but other times, the say is all in how we play our hands and how we choose to interact with the people who matter.

Victor and Hope needed to own their own faults, accept the things they could not change, and man-up to admitting their mistakes. They had to work at letting the past go, instead of rubbing old wounds in each other's faces, which they were famous for doing. Easier said than done, and they both knew they were not ready to just leap into the healing process. They needed time apart, to think, and to truly see and feel what they were giving up, and losing, should they choose that route, though now that seemed impossible. Love was calling them back. Victor had made a decision, for the first time ever, he wanted to quit drinking. He knew, without a doubt, there could be no going back this time. He wanted to save his family, more than anything in the world.

Drinking was not Victor's life path. This had been a temporary phase of ugliness, and he felt awful for all that had been said and done. Perhaps he had experienced a divine intervention of some sort after last night's episode, or he just had a bad taste now, finally, but before he could promise this to anyone, he had to prove to himself. He was so scared to hurt Hope anymore, and surprisingly that suddenly mattered again, like the true Victor was returning. Those were big shoes to fill though, and the question was, did Victor have what it would take to step into those shoes, and would they fit well enough to stay on his feet?

That night, Hope and Victor would relive a segment of their carefree days, as they would talk on the phone, like teenagers again. Really talk. Hope didn't think twice to call Victor at his dad's. For the first time in a very long time, they heard each other. They listened to each other, and they were communicating, and dusting off the cobwebs. They actually had an enjoyable, worthwhile conversation, free from argument, free from stress, and they even managed to smile a time or two during their chatting session. A giggle even flickered its way into the phone, on both ends. The real shocker was that they missed each other, and longed to be together. Their absence, in just a few short hours, had such a huge impact, meanwhile just a few days ago, they could have been miles apart for days on end, and it would have no effect.

Despite their new-found gladness, the couple could not help but retrieve images of their breakdown, and for some reason, this time, the thoughts of their partners' weaknesses was hard to take. They felt so bad, so sorry, so ashamed, yet so willing . . . to push forward and drive on with courage and love. Their emotional fall was a moment of connectivity. They were breathing in a burst of fresh air, in a world so polluted by filth. They were finally taking their lives seriously again, and considering their options, but together, and it felt so good not to fight.

As Hope spoke, Victor engaged in the realisation that he had tuned out the sweetness in her voice for so long. Her voice was soft, like satin. The sweetness that had once melted and weakened him was now projecting through the phone, and he could see the sun beaming from every inch of her body. She wasn't even in the same room as him, but Victor could see her light again. He had been so blinded. This frustrated him now. He envisioned her standing in front of him, an angel, glowing, and reaching her hand out towards him. He noticed her wings were drooping, bent, and fractured, but as he, the helpless lump she was reaching to, down on his knees, reached back, and clasped her hand, her wings transformed. They were instantly mended and shone magnificently. She needed him, and he wanted to be there, to be her hero again, and let her be his angel again.

Victor's vision was teaching him, and he understood that he had robbed Hope of her soaring freedom, but now, here she was saving him, and restoring herself. He understood now that he really was a part of her dreams, a necessary link in her life, and angels cried as they watched the collision of her dreams and his toxicities, the barrier standing in her way. Her broken wings were the result, but with his toxins being cleared away now, her wings were able to heal. The puzzle was solved! She was his God-sent, and together, they could fly! They were necessary to each other. Victor was receiving a message from God, and with that, the angels dried their tears, and smiled.

Hope finally felt that it was okay for her to speak up. She finally felt like she could be open and honest and not shot down for her feelings. They had value, and so did she again, in her own heart and mind. For so long, Hope had felt like the Little Mermaid, staring up into a world that she wanted so immensely, yet it had felt impossibly beyond reach. Unlike Ariel, Hope had lived in her world of wonder, but it had been ripped out of her arms, as she sunk down into the waters below, an even greater pain than the aspiration of an unknown world. Mermaids can breathe in the deep sea, but Hope had been drowning, losing her breath, fading away. Now this little mermaid was receiving her legs, her ticket to the free world, only her voice still existed, unlike poor Ariel in the Disney story. Hope's sacrificing days were coming to an end, finally. Love emerged overhead, and a flicker of hope shone down onto them. She couldn't have felt better if she had won the lottery. This was Hope's million dollar win.

Hope snuck quietly into her daughter's room after giddily hanging up with the words "I love you" ringing in her ears, as if Victor had said them for the very first time ever that night. She spent the next few minutes, just watching her baby, admiring her, and thanking god for sending her to them. She was the perfect combination of Hope and Victor, and she knew they had the potential to do great things, if they worked together, and really set their minds to it. She was indeed their little angel in disguise, sent to save them and guide them, and to show them the true meaning of life. This was all happening for a reason, Hope was sure of that now. This was the true path of their life, and they had just been taught a lesson in appreciation. Just that morning Hope had felt like her world was caving in, now she felt like the world was full of endless possibilities.

"I love you . . . and . . . I love your daddy too", Hope whispered to Gracie.

Some people fly through life much too easily, and with smooth sailing all the way. They cannot understand the hardships of others. They cannot empathize or even sympathize. Whether born into money, good looks, or fame, they just have everything handed to them on a silver platter. Pearls, fancy dresses, limousines, and steak with lobster. In contrast, some people live their entire lives in misery, afraid, unsure, broken, financially disabled, physically crippled, emotionally wrecked, and live a constant battle of challenges. They never get to see the happy side of the globe. For them the world is a dark, lonely, hungry, and tragic place, and they are waiting for the end with every breath they take. These drastic differences that really exist, believe it or not, are just one example of the unfairness of the world. Rich and poor. Happy and sad. Hot and cold. Thick and thin. Fresh and new, or old and dying. Wilting like a flower at the end of the season or blooming with the April showers.

Hope didn't want to place herself in either of these categories, because she wasn't rich and she wasn't poor; she felt average. She could relate though with both sides. She had seen the potential for greatness and happiness, and lived most of her life feeling normal, having ups, and downs, and finding a way through, learning and growing, and making the most of life. Hope had also seen the ugly side of life, and experienced her own unimaginable challenges, which maybe, just maybe could be lessons learned. She was the flower wilting away, but her season was not over yet, and she was being revived and refreshed. A new beginning, a second chance, a beautiful thing . . . all in this moment, Hope was seeing a clear vision, a very powerful feeling.

Hope's intuition told her about Victor's plan to stop drinking, and though she had not heard it from him yet, she knew, and she was already feeling a tidbit of pride and gratitude. She had faith in him to do this. Hope was able to lay in her empty bed, and even smile, as she drifted to sleep, and had sweet dreams. Finally. Sometimes the answers are not right in front of our faces, and sometimes the answers are not spoken directly to us. Sometimes we need to look and dig a little, and other times, we just know. Hope knew.

Victor was ready and willing to attest his love. The storm was over, and the effervescent sun was shining down, like the Grace of God. Victor could no longer live in this false portrait of himself. He knew he could not continue this, his great demise. He had been sabotaging the wonderful opportunity God had placed in his hands. This had been their darkness, just a slight rough patch in their lives.

Issues within a relationship are expected from time to time, but infidelity is an issue within the cheater, and there is no "we" in the ownership of unfaithfulness, at least not where the couple who counts should be concerned. The issues of a relationship do not condone, by any means, the right for one partner to seek out someone new. Maybe these issues make us weak, and help us to justify with ourselves as a cheater, as was the case for Victor, and later for Hope too, but these issues sure as hell do not stand on their own as fair motive. This is often a confused situation, but the partner who strays is at fault, end of story. No excuses, no buttering it up, it is wrong! No 'ifs', 'ands', 'buts', or 'maybes'.

As the offender of betrayal, one must hold accountability. Hope discovered that earlier on than Victor. The partner who was betrayed is the victim of the circumstance. This is setting aside all other setbacks of the relationship, and not jumbling them into the affair. Victor and Hope had both been the victim, and the cheater, each on their own turn, and now they both needed forgiveness and a chance to move on, together.

Even the happiest of marriages can fail, due to raging hormones, and confused emotions. Bad judgement tops off any reasoning though, because if you are supposed to be committed to someone, than morally, there should be no reason good enough to allow this to happen. Alcohol is another weakness that can derange hormones and distort thought patterns. Hope had heard the statement that the truth comes out when a person drinks, but she would argue that fact to some degree. Victor was not a cheater, only the drunken Victor was. Perhaps his own insecurities came out more though when he indulged. Victor was not an asshole, only the drunken Victor was, but again, perhaps he just had less fear and shame with the balls of booze. Victor was a loving man, he had just gotten trapped in the pleasures of booze and the life that came with drinking. Once he put down the bottle for good, he was one of the greatest men on earth, like old times.

Work out the issues, and ignore the flattering attraction or flirtations, politely. Push the temptations aside, and instead work on blossoming the love you already have. Respect that love, respect that person. Let the third party down gently, should the circumstance arise, but let them down, before any misleading is encountered or assumed. Hope would teach Victor to proudly say, "Sorry, you are cute, but I have a girlfriend," and if she, the other woman who may be flirting or hinting, doesn't take that as an answer, get out of the situation, and don't get trapped. Victor would actually listen, and tried this on occasion, and bragged to Hope that he had done well. He had swatted off those hungry mosquitoes out for blood. Hope had learned her lesson, long ago, and she was proud again to admit she was taken. Respect is a powerful tool. Love is even more powerful! Together, they can be unbeatable.

Commitment braches from love, trust, understanding, communication and partnership. The trust is so important, and faithfulness is key to trust. Victor and Hope had unfortunately both been responsible for cheating, and breaking the trust, but it was time to own their faults, forgive, and move forward. The guilt trips, and the self-pity had to stop, and they had to learn to let go, sincerely, with time. They had both gained insight and wisdom, in a miraculous moment, and if they pulled through all this, they would be unbeatable. With this understanding, it was as if Victor was literally washing all the old wounds from Hope's heart and soul, gentle scrubs leaving it fresh and cleansed, to heal.

Communication is a crucial key in love lasting. Hope learned that talking through words, through gestures, through actions, and through our everyday expressions towards our loved ones is such a vital part of survival. Talk about your day, talk about your feelings, talk about your thoughts, your ideas, your dreams, hell just talk about the weather or the cracks in the wall, talk about anything and everything, but remember to talk. The voice of love is huge, and living in silence is no life. Assumption gets us nowhere. If you love someone, tell them, if you are angry, say it, but not in cruelty; and if you have any sort of anxiety or feelings that you feel are important, share them with your partner. "No holding back" . . . that would be Hope's new motto. Love with no boundaries or grudges or fear.

# CHAPTER TWENTY-FOUR

F SOMEONE HAD ONLY been able to pause the scene before Victor and Hope had their little wrestling match that night, the night that changed them forever, and if they could have been shown a TV screen with footage of their future, they probably could have avoided that stupid and senseless night. Everything happens for a reason though; Hope truly believed in fate now. Of course, the "what ifs" can leave us wishing and wondering, but life can not always be great, as human beings we all need some darkness to help us appreciate the light. We need lessons of appreciation and love.

That night must have been necessary, a wake-up call for both of them. They were both heading down disparaging paths and both turning into people they did not like, and they needed that recognition to be laid out for them. Here was Hope's little TV screen tapping into the magical eight ball of her life, and it was saying, "You will find true happiness, so do not give up".

Giving up was not in the books, with one exception. Victor was ready and willing to give up on the bottle of poison, and let loose a bottled up man. He was a genuinely good-hearted man, who had been hiding behind an insecure boy. Maybe he and Hope were not so different after all. He needed guidance, and support, and he found all that in Hope. She herself, lacked direction, but together they would map out a new beginning. Victor's own heart broke as he realised how much he had hurt her, and he wept in sorrow again. He needed to have absolution of all the wrong he had done, this was his time to repent.

His mind and his heart were flooded as he remembered the first moment he knew he was in love, a love like no other, and he knew at that moment his heart was glued to Hope's spirit forever, BUT he had almost thrown all that away, in such recklessness. He would take longer to forgive himself than it would take Hope to forgive him. Victor would recap all the juicy, steamy, heavenly memories that Hope had clung to all this time. Somehow he'd forgotten, in the midst of the booze and anger, but now he clearly remembered and it was a magnificent feeling. Streams and showers of memories, it all felt so new and real again. He was so eternally grateful, and so deeply happy. He could not remember the last time the air he breathed felt so fresh and alive. Angels were singing in heaven, triumphantly, and it echoed right down to earth, right through to his heart.

He fell in love all over in that very second, and he wanted to grab Hope and kiss her as passionately as he had the first time their lips had ever met, many moons ago. He felt a boyish giddiness, and now he knew that he had to put all his effort into making Hope feel loved again. He knew he had to show her what he was feeling, and wipe away all her pain and distrust. He would cleanse his body of all the negative energy, and all the intoxication in his blood, and find virtuousness again. He was so thankful she was still willing to be his side-kick. He was back on her team. They both felt exhilarated, and uplifted.

His freedom of being single was suddenly meaningless, because that was not freedom; that was waste, that was loneliness, that was just fear, and now he knew what truly mattered. Life is what you make of it, he realised now. He had this picture perfect family right at his feet, right at his beck and call, and his for the taking. He had to make the beauty go beyond the picture, he had to make it real. Capture, save, and frame the treasures of his life. He was so blessed it wasn't even funny, and he would be an idiot to reject them and to let them go. He needed to hold dear to them, look after them, and show them the wonders of the world.

Victor had to build up an empire and a legacy to be proud of, and he had to give his little girl a life to be proud of, and most importantly, a dad to be proud of. All his fears subsided, and suddenly he felt capable of anything. He knew that if he hadn't lived this moment, he would have had such deep regret down the road, in five, or ten, or twenty years, and by then it might have been too late, and that was a goose-bumpy feeling. That though alone sent chills oozing down his spine, and he felt like a god-damn fool. He came so close to losing everything, and to having nothing. Alcohol was not worth that. He had to fix the damages while Gracie was young, and repave her future with hope and happiness, and a chance for success and greatness. Victor was excited to see what was to come.

Victor knew that if Gracie had even an ounce of her mother in her, she would be ok, she would do great things, and he strongly believed in her, and in them as a family again. They all deserved better than a life of alcoholism. The only part of that life Gracie would ever know, was through stories, and Victor was determined to make sure of that. The evolution was amongst them now. He was breaking the cycle, and beginning a new legacy that his entire family could be proud of.

Victor could not describe the truly life-changing feelings he was experiencing in just moments. This was larger than life. Everything was spelled out for him, so clearly now. Out of the blue, everything made sense, and he was so moved by the epiphany streaming over him. Finally, he and Hope were back on solid ground, on the same page, and in love. Their souls rekindled. From that day forward, they would live, not always happily, not always in a fairy-tale bubble, but humbly and contently ever after, for even an argument could leave them laughing, cherishing their ability to work through and meet half-way. Compromise, negotiation, and walking towards each other, with open minds.

Dreams really can come true, and nightmares really can end. They had unveiled the silver lining behind the clouds that had been curtaining their dreams for far too long now. Hope had patience, she had passion, she held on, she was strong, despite feeling so weak, and that strength kept her going, and Victor realised she was his guardian angel. He saw her halo shimmering again. She deserved a metal for sticking by him. She helped him to find himself again and to fall in love again, with himself. He had never fallen out of love with her, he had just lost his own soul, but only temporarily thank god.

You really have to wonder, if all the people who get divorced just took one minute to consider how they could refresh a stale love, there might be a chance for them, but too many people miss out on these life-changing moments and give up just a bit too easily. They ignore the moments that could be breathtaking. Hope and Victor believed that love is worth fighting for to the bitter end.

Hope was playing with her daughter one afternoon down the road, when she would experience yet another of her infamous moments, getting lost in her thoughts. She fearfully imagined what her life could have become if it were not for the miracle of the day they found each other again. Unlike the days of feeling envious towards the world, she now knew that there were people so much worse off then her. She might never fully understand how, with a snap, it all fell back into place, like a puzzle, just fitting perfectly, yet in her catastrophic thoughts, she could not help but feel a hint of sadness. She had lived through hell. The sadness of what could have been was a much better thought than a regret of what is. Hope had discovered that we should not live in the past, but instead, we should work for a happy tomorrow and days to come, and let today be a great one, a 'present', everyday! What was becoming of her life seemed beautiful and precious again, as a smile jumped off of Hope's face.

# CHAPTER TWENTY-FIVE

ICTOR GOT HIS DRIVER'S licence back, and with the acceptance and support of Hope, he went back on the road, long-haul trucking. Victor always had passion in being a truck-driver, his childhood goal and dream, just like his dad. It was in his blood, he was a born-trucker. Now that they were intact, Hope wanted him to be happy, and she knew she could not stand in the way of his passion. If he worked from home, and was miserable, what quality of life would that be? Whereas, f they made the most of the time when he was at home, they would be fine. Victor's unhappiness at the job he wound with after losing his licence in the first place was part of his unhappiness and part of the boredom that pushed him further into his rut with booze.

Hope learned her capabilities and strengths to hold down the fort all week, but only with the love and emotional support of a loving partner. Victor was always thinking of Hope and Gracie, no matter how many miles away he was. His passion for trucking faded though, because the highway took him away from his new passion. Each time he had to leave, after being home a day or two, it became harder and harder to walk out the door. Meanwhile, Hope was at home, pregnant with their second child, and the doctor had also recently told her that she needed to slow down and stop working. Being self-employed as a child-care provider out of her home, she had no maternity pay available to her, and they were not expecting the lack of income this early. The anxiety and stress were too much for Victor, and he was tired, and scared, and he started having dizzy spells on the road. He drove himself to the nearest hospital, in fear that he was having a stroke, and evidently, besides a series of testing to come, he again, had his driver's licence taken away. Life works in mysterious ways.

This was no punishment, but it still felt as much, and though this time the loss was for medical reasoning, his livelihood was dependant of this nevertheless. No licence, no trucking job. Maybe this was fate, another of those `meant to be` moments, but that was hard to accept or believe at the time. What it meant at the time was a complete loss of income for the household, neither of them employed, and a baby on the way, plus, a toddler still to feed and clothe.

Hope and Victor were literally struggling in financial crisis, unable to pay bills or buy necessities. Bill collectors were breathing down their neck, calling daily, sending nasty letters, and they were facing foreclosure on their mortgage. The thought of losing everything is certainly a scary thought, but this somehow seemed easier to Hope than the previous year, where she almost lost Victor. If she had nothing, but him, and their family, she really could live on love. This was serious, and they were in major crisis, but they were fortunate enough to have the love and support of a great family, on both sides. Their family members however, had their own needs and bills, and nobody had much extra to give, but Victor's father saved them, lending them mounds of money, thousands of dollars here and there, just to get them back on their feet. Despite his past issues with alcohol, and not always being the greatest dad, he was wonderful to them now. He would never truly understand their appreciation and sincerest gratitude.

Hope secretly worshiped the ground her father-in-law walked on now. He was also a wonderful grandfather, who became known as `Tub Tub`, as little Gracie referred to him. Nobody knew where she had come up with the term, but it was too cute and too funny not to use, and so it stuck and he was from them on known as `Tub Tub`, not only by the family, but the entire community. Oh the power of a child sometimes! Hope loved him dearly, and could never put into words how thankful she was. She shivered at the thought of how bad things would have been without him, and quickly pushed those thoughts aside.

Through this disaster, amazingly enough, Hope and Victor did not allow the stress to drag down their relationship. They endured the stress as partners, trying their best not to point fingers. They had basically nothing, but they still had each other, and their little girl. They were non-materialistic, and luckily never had been, but this was still an adjustment. They had to cling to their family, for they learned the importance of family during the bloodshed of Victor's drinking days and their constant battles. They had to keep some strength and faith, with a new baby in the picture, and now two children to care for.

By sticking together, through the difficult phase, they were able to pull their heads above the water, again not forgetting, with the great help of Victor's dad. Hope had this motto, although she kept it to herself, but it went something along the lines of, "Everything that happens between Victor and I is big, either horrible or extremely wonderful, but always big, never plain, never boring . . . we have a relationship of extremes".

Hope would get right back into the swing of daycare, with baby number two only two months old, and big sister not even two years, and knowing she was a wee bit crazy, but knowing it was necessary, and that she would be ok. Now if a person can keep it together with two kids under two, that says a lot about a person, especially if they do it with happiness and a smile. Doing all that, and more, and juggling a few more kids into the mix, well that deserved an award, if you asked Hope. With time, Victor would find a local job, just what they wanted, and just the answer to their prayers, because now leaving his precious ladies was not so desirable. Not for more than a day or two.

He could pretend, as he drove his big truck locally, morning till afternoon, that he was still a trucker, but when he made it home by supper, and his little girls would light up as he entered, he would be reassured that home was exactly where he was meant to be. With a wife like Hope, and supper on the table, how could he resist the magic of a family. Long-haul trucking, that was a life for single men, and future divorcees, as far as Victor had seen. They were happy with their lives, and they would strive to keep things in line, and to continue paving the way to better, brighter and greater days and opportunities for their family. Now here Hope was, staring into her future . . . all her dreams were coming true—she would get her life-long big wish.

# CHAPTER TWENTY-SIX

HOPE AND VICTOR WERE sitting at a concert, their favourite band was singing a beautiful love song, the one they called their song, and as he wrapped his fingers in a circle around her ring finger, he asked her, "Will you marry me dear?" Sweet and simple, but exceptionally romantic. He didn't have a real ring, yet, due to financial circumstances, but Hope was not materialistic after all, and though she wanted a ring, it didn't have to cost much, or be anything fancy. She would not have asked for a different moment, because his fingers around hers was more romantic anyway. The true meaning of his question was what melted Hope's heart, and no ring could beat the ringing in her ears, his words would vibrate through her. The symbol of any piece of metal Victor stuck on her finger was all Hope cared about.

They both felt tears welling, and could not even hear the words of their favourite song, as it was so blurred by the excitement flaring. It was almost like that moment when he asked her to be his girlfriend, or their first kiss, or their first love-making session. It was a wonderful blend of all those famous first moments they had shared, but this one really took the cake. She could not have asked for a more magical proposal, it was victorious. Fairy tales really can come true! Here they were back to making beautiful memories, living and loving, and having faith. For Victor, of all people to pop that question, heaven itself must be having a party, while the stars aligned, and anything was possible from that moment on, as far as Hope was concerned.

Do you think that any man has the capabilities to turn himself around, and go from wild to tamed, from single schmuk, or `player`, to a family man wooing his wife? Hope was starting to think so. It's in the heart, and in the head, and how we play our cards, as women, and as men, and as a duo. Circumstance could turn Mr. Testosterone who thinks with his penis only, into a sensible, caring and genuine man. Maybe romance novels summarize the story with a little more oomph than reality could produce, but Hope was really starting to believe in this theory. Commitment is like a plague to several men, dreaded and fearsome, but is commitment really defined by signing papers, buying rings, decorating, and dressing pretty, or is it defined by life, by moments, and by love? The moments and how they play out are what really make love count.

Hope always dreamed of getting married, as anyone who knew Hope, probably knew, but she never realised that commitment comes in various forms, and that having babies would be a bigger step than marriage. Most people don't test drive daddies before tying the knot, but Hope had two of the most life-affirming, no turning-back type of commitments. A baby is the most amazing gift that two people can share. Having a baby does not mean you absolutely have to make it work, but it gives a little more reason to strive for success. For Hope, that was important.

When they heard the wonderful news, Hope's parents, felt an overwhelming pride towards both their daughter, and their soon-to-be son-in-law who had filled the title long ago. The truth was, they fell in love with Victor, as quickly as Hope had, which made it more difficult for Hope in the tough times, because she was scared to disappoint them. Their approval was so important to Hope. She respected their decisions, and she knew they were hurt and let-down by Victor's mistakes and drinking habits. She always downplayed the issues, and never had the guts to let them know how ugly their relationship had gotten. It wasn't until the day after their big fight that she finally filled them in. Their instincts had told them there was a distance between Hope and Victor long ago, but they really didn't understand the seriousness. Hope was courageously suffering in silence for quite awhile.

When they heard about the disaster, they were scared for her, and for Gracie, and even for Victor, despite the pain he was inflicting on their daughter. They had an unresolved love for Victor, that they knew could never really end. To see the two of them grow, learn, and flourish was such a relief and an inspiration to them, along with several other family members on both Hope's side, as well as Victor's family members. They were a prime example; an enlightenment! Hope had worried though, with such negativity towards the idea of marriage which circled Victor's family, would he get any hard time from anyone, or would they just be happy . . . and that they were!

That night, as Hope felt more loved than ever, she would make the most profound and sweet love to her fiancé', a word that sounded so goofy in its newness, yet so sophisticated all at the same time. She didn't have to dress it up, or try to make it sensational, because it was just what it was, real and beautiful. Her entire body was on fire, hot and vicious; but with a cuddling by a fireplace in a cozy blanket, on a cold night, type of a comfort. As Victor slept, his body was like a beach-front view, and Hope just wanted to stare at him all night. She felt a need to pinch herself, was this real? He wanted her, and only her, and he was ready to let the world in on that little secret. He had thought this through, and this was really happening, and Hope was so so happy. She had no doubt or question anymore . . . she knew how true Victor's love and commitment to her really was now. In those seconds, when he proposed, she was awestruck. A dream come true.

# CHAPTER TWENTY-SEVEN

OPE COULD FAST FORWARD to her wedding ceremony and it was gorgeous; sunny weather, lake-side on Victor's families' land, a cute little sail-boat floating in the background of their pictures. The music, the flowers, simple and elegant all at once, and it all had Hope and Victor written across the skies; their own fairy-tale wedding. She would be a beautiful bride, who tearfully strolled into the arms of her prince charming, feeling a dreamy enchantment parading around her. Happiness was written all over her, head to toe she glowed with devotion. To be here, it seemed astounding to Hope, phenomenal even, thinking that "life really can bring us miracles".

As she made her way to her future her mind journeyed back, the good and the bad tumbled into her thoughts, the bad only made her more grateful to be in this joyous moment, it was all worth the wait. The good times were more wonderful knowing they paved the way to getting here, and that there were more to come. There was some irony laying in the fact that Hope felt a twinge of gratitude towards the hated bottle she had blamed for so much of their grief, because without that brutal bottle of poison, their relationship may never have been tested so crucially, and perhaps their appreciation wouldn't be as strong today. Patience really is a virtue, and sometimes being foolish is a blessing in disguise. She would wear her new last name like a beautiful ball gown, feeling elegant and proud.

Watching Hope step towards him made Victor feel like a little boy again, on Christmas morning, after just opening his favourite gift. Victor thought Hope was stunning in her dress, and could not be more happy with his decisions. A sand ceremony to symbolize the unbreakable ties that bound them was just one more beauty of the day. Two colors of sand, one poured by Hope, the other by Victor, into a heart-shaped vase, where the grains could never again be separated, a commemorative keepsake they would treasure on display for years to come. Their daughters added a third color of sand to symbolize their present children and any future children to come, and the official union of their family all as one. Macho Mr. Victor was the one who chose this as a feature for their wedding, and Hope was also thrilled by the idea.

The people who mattered most stood up for them, a lovely bridal party, as they stood in front of God, and pledged their everlasting love. They heard wonderful speeches, and saw family all coming together to celebrate, and the groom, a sober Victor who hadn't touched a drop for nearly two years on the day of their wedding was happy to be part of such greatness. He was her prince, he was that groom that she always imagined, and as they danced their first dance as husband and wife, they both felt like they had conquered the world. Hope felt so loved and needed again, and that was an incredibly astonishing feeling! The day was a refreshingly revitalizing day that would be stamped into their memory banks for eternity.

Hope's sister, her Maid of Honour, made a speech that left a mark, because not only was it tear-jerking, but it highlighted the couple's attributes, which many couples lack as time goes on. She pointed out their abilities to still make one another laugh, to have fun, and still enjoy each other's company. It is easy to get caught up in routine and the busy days when kids are in the picture, but Hope and Victor tried almost every day to just say "I love you", not just verbally, but sometimes just a wink, a simple touch, a gesture, or whatever it may be. They had date nights. That is what babysitters are for, or if you are lucky Grandma lives nearby, and enjoys stealing her precious grandbabies, even without being asked at times. The other grandparents, Baba and Gido, Hope's parents, were also quite easily bribed, but that took a little more planning ahead, due to their distance, and the hour-long drive that someone had to make to either pick-up or drop off the precious cargo.

Whatever the case, the couple were lucky to have family around, and certainly didn't lose their lives when they became mom and dad. Their kids only added to the enjoyments they partook in, giving them a new level of life, and expanding their fun! They made sure that despite being parents, they still made time for their relationship to blossom and prosper and live on. Hope's sister admired the couple, and that was something that really hit both Hope and Victor, and with that in mind, they would certainly continue in this fashion. Their children had good senses of humour also, and lit up watching mommy and daddy giggle, dance, and smooch in front of them.

Hope had her chance to be a princess, and everyday after that she looked at her ring finger and those rings were her salvation. She felt like a princess just by the sparkle on her hand, and especially because of the victory they represented, the man who shared her life with her, her newly wedded husband. He too, loved his ring, and looked at it daily, knowing that it was his token of success, sobriety, and sweetness, for he had figured out what Hope meant all those years. He knew that he needed her, and that she was his other half who made him whole. When someone else loves you for who you truly are, as an individual, it makes you want to be a better person. Hope saw this in truth and reality, as a self-liberation. She was able to love herself more again, truly and deeply. She wanted to be a great person for herself, for her daughter, but also for the man who uplifted her and made her feel so good about life again.

Hope could watch the wonderful videos, and relive that beautiful time, wishing she could go back sometimes, but unspeakably grateful to have had that opportunity. She would trifle through the pictures, with such pleasure, but nothing could retrace such a crimson rosy smile on her face, as her own memories, the reiterations her mind could depict, gloriously allowing her to step back and be the bride again, and to get lost in the flashbacks of her favourite day.

The remarkably notable feature of tying the knot for Victor and Hope, believe it or not, was quite opposite to many couples who get lost in the realities of life after marriage, and drift into their own routines and somehow lose sight of one another. Stories of lovers who lose the romance within a year of marriage are too often a norm, and not that these couples get divorced, but they just fall into a rut. Victor and Hope, on the other hand, learned much about love and life and each other before taking the plunge, and by the time they united in holly matrimony, they had grown such a fondness and genuine appreciation for each other. They had been through the era of losing sight, and had now regained their vision and need. They would only allow their relationship to become stronger, and allow themselves to learn to be the best husband and wife and partners they could be. They could even be looked upon as role models, an example of true love.

Some people spend their whole lives waiting and searching for that special someone, while others catch a peek of what they want, but somehow let it slip away, and find themselves asking, ``What if``, ten years down the road, and mourning for what could have been. Then there are the ones who might as well let it bite them, because their soul mate is the boy next door, the waitress at their morning café, or perhaps their best friend, and they just can not push their pride, stubborn natures, and reservations aside, because their fears over-ride the possibility of life-long happiness.

Some people just settle for being content with themselves, even convincing themselves that they are not meant to find love, that they are better off on their own, and not noticing the void. Very rarely, does true love come along, and hit so dead on that you know, especially when the trials of life try standing in the way, but if you can cling to that love, and get through the curves, past the bumps and bruises and capture the sweetness, well then you deserve to feel the magic, just like a fairy tale princess. Remember Cinderella had obstacles too, but she persevered to find and keep her prince. Hope was Cinderella, keeping her cool right in the thick of it all.

They were not salt and pepper, but they were made for each other, it was unmistakable now. Destiny had to have brought them together, to embark on this journey, meant to teach them that people should never be taken for granted, and that love must be appreciated and nourished. It isn't always pretty gardens, butterflies and fairies, or soft-sand beaches; and you cannot spend your days watching sleeping babies, living through them, as much as Hope enjoyed getting lost in the dreams of her daughter. Life is not always a cup of tea or even a glass of fresh, cold, water, but when we look into that glass, what do we see?

Is that glass half empty or half full? When it starts to get empty, do we finish it, dump it out, or do we re-fill it, and re-embark on the purity that once was. The bigger picture is what really matters. Life can throw some deadly curves in the road, but if we tell ourselves we can get around them and that the road is straighter around the bend, we can overcome the difficult times. Hope understood now, she was smart to hang on, despite always feeling like a fool. Deep down she always knew Victor could find his way.

Hope had learned that she had the necessities to take care of herself and be more independent if needed, but Victor was now a man whom she could depend on again, and that was such a safe feeling, which truly put her mind at ease. He was reliable, and he would look after her when she really needed him to. If she was sick and barely functioning as a mother every once in a blue moon, Victor would take charge. He was a wonderful father, and he would get better and better in the husband department. Hope would joke that he was indeed trainable.

Not salt and pepper, but a compromise, a wonderful comprise . . . perhaps she was the sugar and he was the salt, very different, yet many similarities, and when put together properly, well they could be a deliciously delightful treat, complimenting each other just so. Hope and Victor's concoction for love needed the right ingredients though, to be a winning combination. Alcohol was not in the recipe, not even a drop, not a sip, not an ounce, not a taste, not anymore.

Eliminate the deadly poison, and instead, throw in an added touch of tender loving care, and they could be wonderful. Could be, had been, and WILL be. The recipe got scuffled and they were adding the wrong ingredients lately, and not even a goat would take a bite from that atrocious dish. Sometimes when things get thrown off course, it is ok to start over. A fresh new batch, and a scrumptious aroma wafted through the kitchen now, as Hope cooked them a celebratory dinner alongside the remake of their relationship. As she poured them each a glass of pop, they toasted to the fact that they didn't need wine or any liquor to say `Cheers` to new beginnings.

Victor had broken the vicious cycle of his family, and tamed the Maverick side of himself. He could still be a little wild at times, within reason, for it was his individuality that Hope loved. No need to get rid of a treasure, just get rid of the weapons in the treasure chest. Victor was going to prove to the world that marriage can last forever, and that love and relationships are what you make of them. He had a goal that he would make things as close to perfect as he could, from that day forward. He would never take his family for granted again.

The rest of their lives, would be like any life, a risk and an uncertainty, but Hope had faith, and so did Victor, finally. They definitely had choices which they would face and make together, hand in hand, but God also played a hand in the providence of their lives. The unknown is also exciting, if you step in with an open mind.

# CHAPTER TWENTY-EIGHT

JUST WHEN THEY FELT things couldn't get much better, their love would be reinforced again, not without some fears, but so worthwhile, with the birth of another precious girl, Destiny Rae Grant, just twenty-one months younger than her big sister. Handful? Absolutely, but a joyful one, a heart-full, a house-full, and plenty of love and laughter to go around. Hope was so fond of her babies, including Victor and his little sweethearts, daddy's little devilish angels. She would catch herself drifting into awe, as she would watch Victor interact with his daughters and she could see his love for them, all of them, including for her! It was joyous and grand, and nobody would ever be so filled with gratitude for life, every single, god-given day.

Hope was happy and willing to tell their story, in hopes that it would reach people who needed to hear it. She knew that alcoholism plays a role in a huge percentage of lives worldwide, along with infidelity, violence, and all the areas that her and Victor had lived through. She also knew there were worse case scenarios and that she was one of the lucky ones. They were fortunate enough to get past the ugliness and move forward, still intact, and she knew for many, that was not the case. By no means was Hope trying to sell a false sense of perfection, or even false hope that everyone will find their happy ending, if they just hang in there. For some people hope is all they have left, and in times of darkness, when happiness is impossible, isn't it better to cling to a little bit of hope? You cannot help everyone, but for the strugglers and sufferers, Hope believed that there were more

Victors out there, men who are willing to accept and own their faults and strive to overcome them.

Hope needed to be told in the early days of motherhood that it is okay to leave dirty dishes overnight, and a few piles of laundry won't harm anyone. Shutting yourself in a room for five minutes to breathe when you have a cranky baby all day is fine. You cannot ignore the baby all day, but five minutes to keep sane is a secret a mother can use. You cannot keep a diaper wet too long, or starve your baby of nourishment or attention, but the house can wait sometimes. Hope learned all this, with due time. However, her organization skills would increase over the years, along with her household cleanliness and routine for daily chores. Truth be told though, a clean house is not always a happy house, and love can be lost in each scrub. Love is what matters, more than anything; the rest can be sorted out from there. Life is a classroom, and Hope came a long way in just one, two, three years of parenting, as well as with the role of a wife. Learn and grow, learn and grow, but always with love!

Sometimes we have to get it wrong, before we can get it right, but if we take the lessons with us along the way, that's what matters, and that is what life is all about. The true nature in being human lays in our imperfections. What a boring world it would be if everyone was perfect. Where is the uniqueness in that? We all make mistakes. Our ability to admit our faults, and the willingness to say "I made a mistake." Or . . . "I was wrong." Or . . . "I am sorry." That is courage, and that is human.

One morning when she woke, Hope glanced over at Victor, and was instantly consumed by his love, though he was still sound asleep. She remembered through the night, his arms had folded in around her body, and as they slept, snuggled together, she heard their hearts sing a glistening tune. Despite the beauty, Victor did not hesitate to voice his famous line of Hope's body wrapping around his during the night, "like a vine". She was always cold, and his body gave her warmth, glorious warmth that streamed from within and outside too.

She arose from bed that glorious morning, and went to make coffee, and as she sipped at her sweet, creamy brew, she was inspired by the walls around her. This was a perfect moment. The deliciousness of the coffee seeped into Hope's soul, warm and wonderful. Pictures and frames covered the walls of her living room, replacing what was once bare and cold. Their wedding day was preserved and on display, memories for them to cherish each and every single day, to remind them of how far they had come and how proud they deserved to be, of themselves, and one another.

Six months after being married, Hope truly felt that Victor was a better husband than he ever had been as a boyfriend. His down spell as he battled his addiction and the problems of booze were now a positive reminder that in the blink of an eye, things can change. Hope had to be optimistic, and believe that the worst was over, and the only changes now, would be positive, and that she had an angel looking over her shoulder. Her faith in great things was immense.

Forgiveness was a powerful term, starting with Victor, herself, and also the other parties involved in their affairs and mishaps. Hope forgave anyone who was sincerely sorry, and in her mind and heart, things were right. Endless possibilities lurked overhead. Hope would never forget the amazing support that her and Victor were blessed with, including two loving sets of parents, great siblings, and others who would be by their sides through it all! Blessed might not be a strong enough word.

Hope and Victor still argued over every-day life once in awhile. They were young parents, with two small children, close in age, and bills and a mortgage were a constant reminder that they were not kids anymore. That is realistic, a man and a woman will always have differences, but once entered into the union of matrimony, your best friend is the person there all the time, and Hope and Victor had a love that was huge. They were best friends, and they could rely and confide in and on one another. Their love, their family, their children, their marriage, and the growth and commitment that they were blessed with was truly remarkable.

One evening, as they sat back and watched a movie together, Hope would of course have tears streaming down her soft cheeks, in the moment when a man first professed his love for a woman, and though Victor would giggle at her sappiness, he was so thankful for her golden heart. She would not be there, watching that movie with him, and he may still be out binging somewhere, if it were not for her open heart. When Hope's tears turned into a river of sobs, Victor was a bit concerned. He asked Hope what was wrong, and she replied, "Absolutely nothing, that is why I am crying."

After a slight pause, as she composed herself, she whispered, "I have all that, I really and truly have all that." Hope was honestly grateful for her life, and truly felt blessed. She experienced these moments often, triggered by movies, books, songs, or just watching Victor interact with their children, sometimes even just listening to him speak to her. She wore her heart on her sleeve, whole-heartedly living life to the fullest. She had discovered that making sure love is known and never hiding how you feel is so important. She realised the importance of making the most of every breath life blows your way! If she never had more than this, it was enough. A roof over her head, two beautiful daughters, and a man who now proved his devotion each and every day, and all the extras on the side! "Live for the moment", she thought. Those were the words Hope and Victor would live by forevermore, through good times and bad, in sickness and health, for richer or for poorer, till death do them part.

No couple would ever grasp on to their wedding vows with such comprehension and truth as Hope and Victor, for they had lived through it all already, at their young age. They had come out of the anarchy with their heads held high, and they had adapted new values, and morals, and they had discovered the importance of negotiation, comprise, partnership, and communication. They were fully committed to each other, to their marriage, and to their family. To Hope, Victor's proposal and willingness to be married was a confirmation of that ultimate and final commitment. He had come a far way. He knew how important the values of marriage were to Hope. They had a whole new appreciation for each other. There was only room for improvement now. "Seize the day! Carpi diem!", whispered Hope.

Hope found a new sense of peace when the sun went down. The evenings which used to seem so long and dark now gave her a break from her busy days, and where she used to see a black and scary sky, looking out the picture window, she saw a gorgeous full moon shining, lighting up the night. All was calm and just and right in her world. Her home, which once seemed so unwelcoming to her was now a home, with every sense of the word. The walls knew joy, and every room had a story. Those stories were the highlights of Hope's life, of precious moments shared by her, her daughters, and Victor.

In real life, we don't get to flash forward to see how our future will play out in detail. Not unless we believe in fortune tellers, but there is no physical footage on a screen. Reverting back to the hellish night when Victor and Hope reached their weakest feat, most people would imagine that was their last straw. The damages seemed irreversible as events unfolded, in Hope's vision. When Victor packed his bags that day following their ugly, vicious battle; seeming like such a catastrophic waste; most would assume that from there, they just could not overcome the pain. Love should not come at such high cost, and if that had been the end, Hope would have never lived out her full potential of sharing a vibrant coat of happiness with the world. She would have been permanently scarred and changed. That much she knew for certain. Despite their flaws, she knew that her and Victor really did have a special bond, and despite all odds, she loved him so incredibly much.

Hope was starting to believe that her worst nightmare of raising a child in separation was the only option now, as each day seemed worse, and every argument seemed to drive a greater divide between them. She would be lovesick for the rest of her life. That truly was their final breaking point, and they were stripped of their last defences, needing a hand to get back up. Hope and Victor were two of the most selfless people, because stories like this do not come around everyday. The turnaround was so fast, so huge, and so amazing. A fairy tale. Without the poison, they were a team again!

You have to wonder, if you peeled back the layers of fluffy clouds fluttering around up there, above everyone, would you find someone, like a wise old bearded-man, sitting in a big old leather chair, writing? Writing the stories of our lives . . . is every choice we make predetermined or are there just a few select outcomes that are inevitable, despite the shuffle of paths we choose? Families, lovers, friends . . . are they matched with us at birth? Hope pondered, "does anyone hear our prayers?" . . . she thought so.

To forgive and push forward, giving themselves and each other a second chance took courage, and although Hope felt foolish at times, maybe she really was a psychic genius with genuine intuition, to know that if she had patience, love would win. Maybe she secretly had no control, and a higher hand was leading her. She had the right to rub it into everyone else's faces, to all those who ever doubted hers and Victor's true love, but of course that was not like Hope. Those people were just being rational, but Hope was okay with living a life that was not predictable or clear cut and that defied the odds. Hope and Victor would never forget that ugly night, the worst of many ugly nights, but they could be proud that their story did NOT have a different ending. They could and would be proud of their happy ending, or . . . their happy new beginning. A second chance. Remember, love doesn't always make sense, and it can be messy, but true love never fails.

# THE END

# About the Author

Jennifer Lynn Brown is a small town girl, who enjoys the simplicities of life, raising her beautiful children, along with husband, Richard, and just trying to make the most of life and love. Brown believes herself to be an optimist, feeling that when life brings us down, we must sweep off our knees and get back up. There is always someone worse off, and looking at the brighter side of life can make all the difference in how we play our next hand. Brown's book is based on the real life events of a couple who lived through the drama portrayed in this story, in the early days of young motherhood and a tainted relationship, cursed by alcohol. Readers may find this story a self-help tale of victory and hope, through the characters of Hope and Victor.